My Name is Henrietta Rose

a novel by

Barbara de la Cuesta

Finishing Line Press
Georgetown, Kentucky

My Name is Henrietta Rose

Publisher: Leah Huete de Maines

Editor: Christen Kincaid

Cover Art: Barbara de la Cuesta

Author Photo: Constance Pilling

Cover Design: Elizabeth Maines McCleavy

Order online: www.finishinglinepress.com
also available on amazon.com

Author inquiries and mail orders:
Finishing Line Press
P. O. Box 1626
Georgetown, Kentucky 40324
U. S. A.

*In gratitude for monthlong fellowship
to Ragdale Foundation where this book began*

I

Memories of childhood, in Henrietta Rose's case, were pleasantly intact.

The corridor passed from the enormous, old fashioned kitchen with the table painted blue in the center—so large you couldn't imagine it coming through any door, perhaps the house was built around it. Then a series of little rooms containing linen, Christmas decorations, outgrown toys, and mops and brooms, to the narrow service stair, which went steeply up two turns; You glimpsed the Chinese red dining room through wavery glass, and past the little bedroom where Nummy slept when they were little; and later Hulda Enbretsen, the cook, slept.

Once, when Henrietta was very young, it disappeared, the corridor, the stairway. And no one to tell it to or help her...Mounty in the hospital, having out his adenoids, to prevent recurrence of those sinus infections that almost carried him off like the remote older brother, Pierce, she'd never known. Mounty saved by newly discovered sulfa drugs—or could have been the adenoid removal. He was never sick again. Nor she.

When he came home, the corridor reappeared. They resumed predations on the kitchen, carrying up uneaten bowls of oatmeal, cups of chocolate, bowls of raw oats or rice—Mounty responsible for these more difficult thefts. Coffee grounds and teabags—used; or, from a medicine closet: toothpaste, pungent liniments, eucalyptus smelling salves. These thrilled her most; they seemed to her most likely to provoke the chemical reactions they were after...

Past Hulda's room, another stair, no turning to it, steeper, to a fourth floor, finished but unused, sometimes Mounty, but usually she, who had a growing reputation as a finicky eater, was the one to sneak food especially past Inez from the Canary Islands, Hulda Engbretsen, the cook.

And then along another corridor, with peeling wallpaper, of hunting scenes, a closet with a raised shelf meant for shoes: Here they kept the many bowls and spoons and one great crock, into which Mounty sometimes let her measure in the latest ingredient, hopefully the one to roil and transmute the mixture.

Into what? In later days when they could read, it was, she guessed, to gold. Base elements to gold. For they were alchemists by then. Or Mounty was. Much cooler and more logical than she. The roiling to her, somehow connected to the danger undergone, the theft, itself, the catalyst. And the hoped-for product— for her, she now knows—was not gold, but rather some organic mystery, to be revealed only after the long desired explosion.

II

More recent memories, not so much.

On November 3, in the year of 1983, Henrietta wakes in her HUD subsidized apartment on Locust Street in Waltham, Massachusetts, and, following some instructions pinned to her kitchen cupboard, makes herself some tea and toast with marmalade.

> Tom at 10

Her date book reads. Eight AM, November three.

She might well have also written the following:

> My name is Henrietta Rose...
>
> I am an alcoholic...one drink away from, blah blah blah and all that stuff.
>
> I am seven years five months, and I am not sure how many days, sober. I depend on my notebook to remember this.
>
> Two of my children have disappeared.
>
> One has died.
>
> Another lives in a trailer on a rocky mountainside in New York State.
>
> I live in Waltham, Massachusetts—city of French Canadian, and Irish, and Sicilian, and Central American immigrants, and computer engineers, and madmen released from the Metropolitan State Hospital—in a HUD subsidized apartment on Locust Street.
>
> I attend the Sunshine Club three days a week, a socializing program for the mentally infirm.
>
> I grew up in West Boylston, twenty miles west of here, where my brother Mounty still lives and drinks in the decaying family house of the Montague-Pierces. I was going there to live with him after my daughter died, when I discovered I could not stand up. They took me off the Baltimore and Maine and put me in the Waltham Hospital, and here I remained.
>
> I, Henrietta Rose, was a famous hostess in foreign capitals, known for my conversation and my imaginative parties.
>
> Now I am a sought-after speaker on the circuits of Alcoholics Anonymous. On Thursdays I paint in a naïve style at a free class held in the basement of Christ Episcopal Church.
>
> I make the coffee and replenish the stale cookies and set out the framed portraits of Bill Wilson and Dr. Bob at the Step Meeting Friday noontimes in the basement of the Italian church. I do not seek any higher responsibility than

this.

All these facts she does still remember, though one or two of them sometimes escapes her, as do the events of the previous day or hour even. The Korsakoffs. Its onset was the reason she couldn't stand or walk that day on the train on the way to Mounty's.

No, She doesn't always quite know who she is until she reads her datebook, or quite who this Tom is either; but, looking out the kitchen window, sees him; fifteen minutes early, down in the drive; he's plastering another bumper sticker: HIGHER POWERED to his pumpkin colored pickup's crumpled flanks. He won the raffle Friday noon—she would remember were it not for her affliction—and also a poker chip for one week sober. Really oughn't ride with him...oh but she's not in a position to be fussy. She takes her canes with her, creeps down the stairs.

Ten days and seven hours, fifteen minutes, sober, he tells her, straightening up and looking at his watch.

That's mahvelous Dahling, Henrietta, acting her grand self. He's neatly shaved, has shoveled out the bottles that were rolling round behind the cab.

HIGHER POWERED.

She approves this kind, that make a joking reference to the deity, and yet no disrespect. She saw one once:

JESUS CHRIST IS COMING

...and is he ever pissed,

that made her laugh, and yet it spoke a message, kind of...

I like to win these, he tells her as he straightens. Make the brothers and the sisters honk and wave.

Ah, yes...Yes. She struggles into the high seat, and stows her canes. She has seven years herself; she can remember that. Seven years without the booze. They bump, in the high cab, around the Common, over railroad tracks, out Oak Street, whirl into the parking lot behind the mushroom-shaped St. Joseph's, known as the Italian Church. He helps her out and tenderly hands her canes.

Monday morning at St. Joseph's Rectory is a raw sort of meeting, not so bad as Loony Noony at the Club Surrender, but the tattoo crowd is represented well enough. It's Artie speaking when they enter, slightly late. Sleek, good looking Artie. He's not one who woke up morning after with an unexplained tattoo, but could have been. He's talking about South Boston, Jack Daniels behind the project dumpster, drugs. It's hardly Henrietta Rose's world... She saw him last, of course she can't remember, at a commitment to the detox; he was wearing bath robe and foam slippers. Back where he started from; but he looks good today, sounds chastened. Who'd have bet a nickel on his chances, classic, classic slum kid. "A classic dipsomaniac," that subtle gentleman in a Newton Big Book meeting called her, turning toward her his hooded eyes and interrupting some rubbishy plea of hers that Henrietta Rose was not just any drunk. Who, for that matter, would have bet on her? Not she. He's going to make it, Artie, Yes, she thinks, his eyes are moist, his voice a little shaky, skin as soft and dewy as a newborn. How his mother must exult, she thinks. A mother herself of four, one dead, two fled; and one most likely frozen to death on this winter day of mercury in the teens.

It must be in the tens there in the upper reaches of New York state, where her oldest, Charles, is attempting to live in a trailer on that stony parcel of land he's buying—mostly with her loans. No, not freezing! She wills it in a little prayerful breath, not freezing, God. The rest she doesn't ask. For the rest, she must try to accept that he's still living out some meaning to her, some suffering he must undergo.

But is his suffering, his life, simply for my edification, for my finding painful meaning in it? How cruel. How cruel for him. She wishes Charles could be where Artie is. But the pain it takes, the pain it would take, I won't allow. Not now. Not so soon after Carol. I will send him another check. Not so soon after Carol. I am so weak.

She came back less than a year ago after Carol and only now can she hobble a bit, mostly clinging to a walker, and on good days a cane. When she got off that train...when they took her off that train, limbs, mind, everything had failed her. The Korsakoff's. The Korsakoff's can hit you after years not drinking: It isn't caused because you're sober, dear, explained the nurses. It's because you drank.

She'd been to Plum Island with Carol's ashes, tossing them into the withdrawing froth, and then in Boston a night with Jeannie, and in the morning Jeannie put her on the Boston & Maine to Fitchburg. To Mounty in the big house in West Boylston where they'd grown up.

The last part never happened. She recalled the train was cold, or perhaps it wasn't, was only her weakness after those ten months with Carol on the road... In any case, she'd tried to stand up, pull her coat down from the rack, and her legs had failed her. An evanescence like one of Lutie's famous... She never when she was drinking ever failed so totally.

Korsakoff's disease. They bundled her off the train in Waltham. Here, where she'd remained, a month in Waltham Hospital, two in a nursing home, and now in subsidized housing. They send her Monday, Wednesday, Thursday, to the Sunshine Club, day center for mentally afflicted. Not what she'd have chosen; but her legs are getting stronger with the Irish nurses pulling and pushing at them. Not her mind, however, in spite of mental exercises. A portion of unreeled time is automatically erased. The Korsakoff's.

Affects the short-term memory. The condition, explained the doctors, present all along, although she didn't know it, like one of those World War Two torpedoes the Gloucester fishermen kept netting twenty years after.

Childhood memories were pleasantly intact: The big house in West Boylston, where she and Mounty...where the very corridors were known to disappear, where their mother, Lutie's, evanescences...her upturned pumps the bottom of a stair...

Oh, yes. And then the other theft: The years of her children...ah! When did they menstruate, when sprout pubic hair? When make that subtle turn against her? But these were gone because of blackouts. The years in Venezuela, India... gone. Oh, there are clearings in the fog: a picnic, San Mateo; herself atop an elephant...

Artie's finished. A salvation story. Yes, we are the saved, she won't deny it. Those years of her salvation, too, are intact on the reel: Those early meetings, Troy, and Albany. She went on foot and bicycle. She was so strong. And Carol's illness, operation, hope and hopelessness, and hope again, and setting out to find another doctor, clinic...

John K., middle aged and jaunty, speaks. She doesn't listen, thinking about Charles. She thinks that she can manage another hundred for the gym he wants to join, and that way he can shower, maybe find it possible to get a little job and be all right a month or two...And she, free to pursue her little happinesses...

Oh, one can happy at her age, if only one's children will allow. They tell you don't project on the future. She does it shamelessly all the time, and right in meetings, where she's supposed to be attaining serenity and strength to stay sober another twenty-four hours. Yes, bad for her, to dwell on Charles. If only she was ignorant of where he was, he'd be like the others then; she hardly thinks of them, of Charlotte, Kate...

John K is telling of the romance he had with detoxes. Thirteen, he'd sampled: Get a couple valiums in you, you don't feel too bad, ha ha. You stick your collar up outside your robe and open up a couple buttons—show your chest hair, saunter on down to the dayroom...I mean I'm not talking even about the great ones: Spofford Hall...the lake the mountains...or the Betty Ford...I had a friend got in there...like getting into Harvard...I mean the County, all my stupid plan will pay for. Even at the County, I didn't get it till they threw me out and there was nothing left but you folks, meetings in cellars. Laughter.

Yes, she could be happy maybe if like the others he'd disappear. Or die, like Carol. Oh no, the pain, the pain of Carol... Carol wanted, wanted life, her work her art; and wanted her, her mother,.Henrietta Rose. She hadn't, like the others, given up on her mother. If Carol would rest...she was as restless as that roiling surf she'd thrown the ashes into at Plum Island. A place Carol loved above all other places.

They're standing now to close. She takes the woman's hand on her right, and Tom's on her left and prays out loud with the rest of them. They call it the "Our Father," being Catholics, most of them, but add the Protestant "Kingdom and the Glory." The hand on her right is warm, on left is cold. He's been outside to have a smoke, Tom.

Oh Jesus, I...identifying like hell, about those detoxes. he tells her when they are back in the cab of his truck. The attention's what you need to grab. I think that none of us ever had enough attention, why we do it. They swirl out of the parking lot. It's spitting snow now. I Remember once I went into a church, Tom tells her, right after service, went up to this priest—I thought he was a priest; they told me later he was a Protestant. It was in that big white church downtown. Down on my knees to him, right after mass, or whatever they call it, Protestants…I'm making this big scene so they would put me in a hospital. Big red haired guy, he was. He actually came to see me later in the hospital.

Too cold to sleep outside that night, is why I did it; I knew that; but, just as much I needed the attention. Like a movie scene. I planned it out. You think I should apologize to him? I mean I even thought they might send me to the Betty Ford.

She laughs. Well, maybe not. You ought to leave apologizing till you're more established, she adds, from her present wisdom. And don't have bad thoughts toward yourself. Not at the beginning. They can ruin everything. No, don't apologize.

He drops her at the Sunshine Club.

Today is Thursday, November twelve, says Bertha Bechtel. Snowing slightly, Henrietta adds. Next holiday's…Thanksgiving! Bobby, who is simple, shouts.

Reality Orientation, it is called. A sort of kindergarten, enjoyed by likes of Bobby, Bertha. Supposed to aid her memory, in Henrietta's case.

Rebecca, who directs this, has that widespread professional optimism, puts Henrietta in mind of a therapist she entertained with stories back when she was drinking. Never told a word of truth to the woman in more than five years.

Really, she ought to have written a book instead of wasting everybody's time. And the woman believed her! That was the amazing thing.

Lunch at the Sunshine Club is chicken ala king and instant mashed, Jello salad with peaches. It amuses Henrietta Rose to imagine the grayish peas back in their green pods, potatoes back in their earthy skins, peaches in their fuzzy jackets.

Later they go out to shop for birthday party Monday. They all hold hands to cross DeFinis Street, the very corner, Bertha tells them for the fifteenth time, where she was hit once by a speeding car. Her name was in the paper, she tells them for the fiftteenthh time. They have to wait for Henrietta, clumping with her walker. Becky makes her take it; really she could do without. Frosting, birthday candles, plastic letters and a clown head for the decorations. And banana muffins rolled in nuts for each. She eats hers slowly, feels a lovely contentment, almost, with her day. Who was that nice boy took her to the meeting? Tom, yes, Tom. They had a lovely time, a lovely conversation, she remembers, has forgotten content.

Back again. They set her at her harp to play, "I Dreamnt I Dwelt in Marble Halls," and "Danny Boy," which Bertha, warbles, clutching her patent leather pocketbook to her breast.

Then Becky takes the chart out: one more Orientation to Reality. Henrietta wonders sometimes, does it matter? Should they care a jot what time it is, what day, and if the sun is shining?. Seems to tickle Bobby, especially the part about the next holiday. He knows what Christmas means, the Santa part at least. To her it chiefly means she'll have to sink an extra hundred in that stony lot in New York State.

She's tired. Calves taut, walking on her toes by time the van comes, takes them home. A little snow is still falling. It was like coming home from school in West Boylston, in winter.

III

The explosion never came, though the roiling was accomplished, and the smells became ever more provoking and exciting, reaching to at least a floor below, alerting Hulda Engbretson and the Canary Island Inez, who was forever holding her nose near the staircase and complaining, *Huele. Huele raro*. Oof. These "experiments," as Mounty taught her to call them, kept her in a state of hysteric fear and expectation, that truly made her feel the breakfast nausea which explained her never finishing a bowl or cup of anything.

Mounty read books on alchemy from a shelf of books in the attic which had belonged to an uncle who lived with them for a time. He went mad before she was born, and went to live at the Metropolitan State except for holidays when he stayed with them and slept in Nummy's old room. The ingredients called for in these books were largely unavailable to them, except for rainwater, wine— albeit unconsecrated—salt, and the mercury out of broken thermometers. But the rituals could be carried out. They knelt approaching their messes, Sun and Moon, Artifex and the Soror Mystica, left hands linked, silken rose held commonly in their right...Oh it was thrilling, her part in it utterly necessary, she knew, though Mounty wouldn't acknowledge it, or even show her the pictures in the book. She knew she was the Soror Mystica.

The Mystic Sister, without whom there was no transubstantiation.

One awesome occasion left no doubt of it. You must pee in it, he told her as they stood over the mess.

No, no, I can't! It's disgusting! she cried, but she knew she could. She knew that, aside from being disgusting, the request was thrilling. He must leave the room then, she insisted. He did, and she squatted and provided the urina puerorum, which actually should have come from a boy.

But the boy was disgusted from that day forward, though the request had come from him, and she had docilely filled it; and the Artifex and the Soror Mystica no longer linked left hands and grasped the rose. It's no use, he said. When there's no way we can have a fire to boil it. So, after that, it was she alone who tended the seething, organic mess, while he turned his restless boy's attention to the inorganic, the obdurate and architectural. He grew crystals. Salt and sugar's preservative qualities were discovered. He collected rocks. He became fastidious about his person.

IV

A pristine page, the datebook. She has nowhere she's supposed to be today, but is able to ascertain by various means that it is Saturday, November 16. A sunny day, and windy, the wind rattling the porch screens. The little snow of sometime last week melted, causing the grass between the buildings to revive a tender green. Her name is Henrietta Rose, she knows. What else? Some exercises she must do, to get her heels down on the earth again, extend achilles tendon. She takes a turn without her cane, round the kitchen, sink to chair to table, puts out the tea things, jam and scones they sell now in the IGA. Having tea is an organizing principle to her day. She toasts one of the scones, squirts on the liquid margarine she's told to use. There's a man, whose name she can't remember, blowing leaves before him into the gutter... Cat! A cat, he brought her... yes, she owns a cat, who's absent. Where? Ah! She finds the poor creature closed between the kitchen and the storm door. He must have come in with the upstairs tenant, got in one door and not the other.

Darling, I forgot you. How could I forget you? And I think I brought these creamers...yesterday? Especially for...Here, I put them in the icebox...come, my own, you drink this.

Cat, an orange marmalade, a male, they're always male, and stay-at-homes, they can't be bothered with the rutting and the howling, if you pamper them enough, resemble drowsy retired bankers hardly out of kittenhood... stockbrokers. Always she has had them, since the children. One after another, as they perished under autos, minds distracted by stock prices, presumably, they hadn't any street smarts for all their sagacity in other matters. She came home once, found Carol, who she'd left in charge of everything as usual, finishing up a grave she'd dug behind the drive where a bittersweet bush grew wild. A grave for one of these beloved cats. She must have been no more than twelve, for they were living in that rented house, on route 62, which took a special toll of cats, and also a lovely dog that she remembers.

She remembers, as if before her now, her daughter's face, the look of premature adulthood. And yet she had the sunniest nature; it was why they all made free with her.

But she was only a little girl. If she'd been pressed she would have cried over that cat. But I didn't press her. I couldn't bear to press her, because I was so cowardly. I couldn't bear their pain along with my own. Yes, even now, I can't bear their pain.

There wasn't another cat, although the crippled dog lived on. No, not another cat till you, she says to him. I can't remember what I named you,

Henrietta Rose confesses to her cat. Those early marmalades were all named Mono... The word meant blond in Venezuelan vernacular, where the first Mono came to live with them. For old times' sake she named this one Mono for a day, and then she'd changed it.

Geoffrey. Yes, it comes to her. Geoffrey. You are Geoffrey. There was a poet she liked. Mad. Began a poem "When I consider my cat Geoffrey..."

Yes. She considers him a moment, while he considers her with sea green eyes.

V

When she and Carol got on the train to Seattle, they found four empty seats and spread themselves a bit: their novels, Carol's headset radio, her teddy bear: Single girl again, she finds her comforts, Henrietta thought. For Jason had left her then, and taken Owen, who like Carol was in the hands of doctors

Doctors, doctors. The clinic in Boston had taken out the remaining ovary and a piece of a lung, then sent them to Seattle for some trials with that drug came from a tree. The trees were in Seattle...? No, she had that wrong, but still it stuck in her head. In any case, poor Carol had to heal a bit; there was no hurry, so they took the train, determined to enjoy the view, the dining car. Henrietta, hoping to recapture romance of train trips to Indiana in her girlhood when the wartime trains were full of soldiers, sailors, and there were silver finger bowls on white linen.

It wasn't the same, but rather a slow journey across the northern states, making inexplicable stops in stubble fields, and opposite auto graveyards, backs of houses. There were more stately pauses in the cities of the Hudson valley. Albany, that whited sepulcher. West, then, along the Mohawk valley: river, highway, railroad, parallel for miles. At the foot of overlooking hills, the ugly gothic mill towns with their idle stacks, the rusted locks of the old canal.

They stared out at it for long periods, and then back into their books. What was she reading? Something about science, and the future. Looking there as everywhere for hope of cures, she sees it now.

And then long walks to the dining car, stepping into breach between the cars, and hopscotching over the shifting plates of corrugated steel, Earsplitting rattle, whooosh of another door, then silence, down another aisle, delicately walking hands along the seats...Carol graceful in her leotard. You'd always know she was a dancer. Even ten years after giving it up to take up breeding, brooding, Owen.

And the nights of disarray, of sleepers, under coats, and hitched up skirts and sweaters, night breath, smell of browning apples. They were not among the sleepers. Carol wouldn't take a sleeping compartment first of all. Henrietta had begged her: But I wouldn't sleep, she'd said.

And so, at night, they talked, began to talk, and Henrietta breathed, I'm sorry. into the snoring dark.

You needn't be, Carol said.

Yes, I need be. I need be.

All right. She understood.

And you. You need. Henrietta pursued it. There was a cat once, one of the many we named Mono…

I remember every one of them.

Well, they've all become a blur to me, but I'm talking about the one that was hit by the car on Route 62.

There were two of them. Carol said with that precision with which she had always countered her mother's vagueness.

Ah, well, one of them, I remember you buried in the back yard. I came home and saw you needed to cry, and I wouldn't let you.

I remember.

Of course, it was the drinking… Henrietta continued.

But I never saw you drink.

I took pills. She tells her audience at the Loony Noony. Noon meeting at the Club Surrender downtown.

In the middle of her organizing tea, Tom had appeared down in the drive and honked until she took herself out to the porch to see what was the commotion. But I didn't write anything down, she told him.

I just decided to go, he said. And thought to pick her up. It seems he's taken up her cause, or thought she might take up his.

OK, she said and got her canes, and now she's here and they've asked her to speak, which delights her.

Yes, I took pills. We lived in places where you could just walk in pharmacies and buy whatever. And I drank, of course; but with the pills you could disguise your drinking, and you didn't need to drink as much.

The Loony Noony doesn't mind a straying onto drugs, forbidden topic in most other places. The people at the Loony Noony sit in corners of the Club Surrender like the victims of a bomb, They bring their lunch in paper sacks or eat the cookies and drink the coffee loaded with sugar; their tear-stained children crayon quietly in corners, under tables.

These pills I bought in pharmacies—you could, without a doctor's… I looked things up in medical books; for years I took a major tranquillizer. I liked word "major." But it was the "minor" ones that did the trick I found out later. Thought I was so smart…I didn't think that something minor'd make a dent in the despair I felt.

She's a popular speaker at the Loony Noony, Henrietta Rose. They like it when she uses her grand voice…well after all it is her voice…She forgets that sometimes in this city where she washed up…among the Irish and Italians retired from the Mill, *Le Watch*, the French Canadians who come and go, the Puerto Ricans, who also come and go, because they can. Who would think that Henrietta Rose, who used to think herself a superior type of drunk, would end up here? Slumming, her old friends would have called it. Actually, she's become a kind of clown, and her audience loves it and so does she.

Oh, I was very grand. I had these houses built behind great walls, and gave these parties where the hired musicians played till four or five am, and stretched out on my lawns to sleep it off till afternoon. A little man would come from *la farmacia* at four or so, to give me an injection that I thought I needed to recover from these extravaganzas.

Henrietta's extravaganzas, people called them. Thought I was so smart. Until, one day I looked at the bottle I had finished. Gran Marnier, if you know what that is...bottle that took forty years to age, and I had finished it in twenty minutes. Told me something. Then, another day, I found myself in bed, strange room, oh, mine, my guest room. Wouldn't have been so bad, except I had a guest, my husband's father...I was in his bed. I'd gotten up to the bathroom in a blackout, turned in there...

He wasn't there thank goodness, gone to visit a college friend,.but the potential for embarrassment.... She pauses for effect.

Yes, the potential for embarrassment...when one is a great lady, as Henrietta Rose was then, one can't proceed with this, this...potential for embarrassment, that I knew. I wasn't too far gone to know that.

And so on. It was her standard talk with variations. Partly, it was for Carol.

VI

Tuesday: paint, she's written in the datebook.

Her happiest day. Being happy is a duty she has set herself. Not always easy, because of Carol's lusty ghost, because of Charles. But she lets nothing spoil her Tuesdays. If the phone rings she doesn't answer, in case it's Charles.

On Tuesdays, Henrietta Rose is fetched by city van at ten and driven to the site of the old Sunshine Club on Prospect, basement of The Episcopalian Church. On this day, The Kisser, a local character, probably released long ago from Metropolitan State Hospital, is outside sweeping the steps and wearing one of his outfits, a Red Sox uniform. He has other costumes, among them a colonel's uniform.

She practically steps into his arms as she gets off the van, an event he dreams about all day; and, of course, she is kissed lengthily on her lips. It's happened before, though she avoids it when she can, as do most of the women in town. Then, with the soft impression of his lips on hers, she slips inside and down the basement, a large room that smells of choir robes and yellowed anthems.

Here, she finds a battered easel, a tray table to hold the china plate, one of the set of chipped ware salvaged from a trunk she stored in Natick after Gerald's death, and gleefully squeezes pthalo blue, alizarin crimson, cadmium yellow, and ocre and umber, burnt and raw onto her plate.

Then, on a piece of Masonite, she spreads a coat of all of them together, whirled and swirled: celestial tones at top, and a foundation of burnt umber below.

What's so funny? Warren asks, noting the little smile left over from the kiss perhaps, or simply the pleasure of paint.

She looks like someone getting lots of sex, says Mike O'Sullivan, who is painting every feather of an immensely lifelike pheasant.

A little more respect there, Warren warns. Warren is winding up for one of his flights.

Yeah, yeah, yeah, rumbles Mike.

Henrietta scratches in the thick impasto with the handle of her brush, a tree, with a peculiar pair of horizontal limbs as thick as ponies' bellies, and then the house with the complex set of roofs that's been appearing in all her paintings lately. She doesn't fuss with the perspective.

A veritable nun. Warren goes on: One of those Maryknoll kind. He finds her virginal, some reason. And Bolshy. She used to make Bolshy comments at her cocktail parties, there in that high plateau in Sogamoso, where an

14

occasional Peace Corps worker mingled with her husband's engineers. Just to shock the engineers. She doesn't think she's made them since she caught on to Brezhnev.

Some nun, she says. I was just given a kiss on the lips.

Caught you, eh? The Kisser.

Yes, a rather nice kiss, actually. Soft and...

Sex, just what I said, says Mike.

She's scratching rapidly, a pair of children, gathering acorns under a tree, a soup pot with a fire under. In the tree, another child, female, straddles a fat limb. A horsehead, with a flying mane, is hidden high in the branches. At the top, a male child loops a pulley and another opens an umbrella and prepares to jump.

After the fermentations and the *urina puerorum*, Mounty became fastidious about his body and turned his restless mind to hard things like his rock collection and to physics: Falling bodies, hers and his, were tested from the heights of trees, the many roofs accessible to their bedroom windows, the opposition to gravity of their mother's flowered parasol, their father's several sober black umbrellas, unfurled at precipices...

As always, she'd followed Mounty, even dreamed of perpetual motion apparatuses, broken her ankle in a daring experiment: A silk umbrella turned inside out. But she remained also faithful to the chemistry, the organic. She secretly attended to their experiment, which had begun to smell pleasantly like green apples.

Odd, that she had married Gerald, a chemical engineer. The Alchemist, she'd called him when they were in college.

You had a husband? Warren asked her once.

Of course I did. I had four children.

Warren's bemused. As she'd already noted, he thought her solitary, nunlike. Warren is a secular Jew, which makes this odd. He used to work at the old Bleachery, a hotbed of Bolshies, before he went to college on the G.I. bill to study painting. One of his Polish grandfathers was a painter, and Warren looks astonishingly like the aging Picasso.

And what did this husband do?

He was a chemist. He invented a way to make tortillas with an instant mix. Before you had to boil the corn kernels overnight, then grind them in the morning. He worked four years to duplicate them.

You don't say.

When he finally got it, we gave it to our cook to try. Too complicated, she said, she liked the old way. Now it's on the market; you can get it at the IGA.

You had a cook?

Oh, everybody had a cook. It meant nothing about you.

Hell, you say...says Mike.

Even the servants had servants there.

So, what, then, told people you were rich? Warren asks.

Oh, maybe certain clubs.

And you belonged to them?

Well, I suppose. They didn't tell anything about your class, but maybe about your money. People were frightened and clung together. Made me ashamed. If I went back now, I'd rebel. I'd sit in the cafes, talk politics, ignore the married women. Even then, I did a little. Some people hated me; the higher up a man was in his company, the more I couldn't stand him. At cocktail parties I hung about with the new hires and the Peace Corps people. Gerald felt I held him back in his firm. The wives were supposed to cultivate their husbands' bosses.

And you didn't?

Well, I went to bed with one of them," she tells him to disabuse him of his notions. But that's not what they meant by cultivating.

What a dame!

And now I'm painting in acrylics in a Red Feather Agency for indigent elderly in Waltham, Massachusetts, and kissing crazy people in the streets.

And this husband and these children...

Two of them are fled and one is dead. A very checkered life, I've had.

And the money?

Well, I spent a lot, my daughter's illness, then my son...and who knows who else will come along and need it. So I leave it in my brother Mounty's hands.

And where is he?

West Boylston. I was on the Boston & Maine, on my way to him the day these legs gave way...

And so...Why don't you get back on the train?

She laughs; he's first person ever asked her that.

The last time she saw Mounty… She can't recall the date, but remembers the parlors, the great kitchen of the house, in West Boylston, blocked with old dresses, offset presses, cranberry bins, ancient linotype machines, cookie tins and breadboxes, toppling piles of books, and sloping avalanches of old *National Geographics* on the floor in corners of the rooms. He was running a newsletter for people wanting to exchange collections of Ironside Tapes for books by Tasha Tudor; vintage gas ranges; for horror comics, antique cradles, Shirley Temple dolls, antique soda bottles, English license plates, and all of it passed through the house, which he hardly ever left.

His air of brisk business would have fooled her if she hadn't stayed around to see him subsiding like the piles of magazines into a stupor in late afternoon. She was in one of her early, lost, attempts at sobriety, and talking more about it than she should, and tried to tell Mounty that he could get it back: the wife, the daughter, job on the Exchange…if only he could stop the drinking; but that Mounty of the job on the Exchange she had really experienced very little, being in foreign parts so long. That Mounty couldn't be recalled; instead, she seems to recall encountering the old Mounty of her childhood, that she actually heard him try to interest her on a text on *alchemy*.

No, she probably dreamed this; but his talk of his swapping activities—the swapping newsletter—had something redolent of perpetual motion machines, of the conversion of base matter into precious…

If I were to go there, I probably couldn't get in the door, she says to Warren. Did you ever notice how the disorder in some people's houses reflects some terrible disorder in their minds, their psyche?

Warren shrugs. He thinks she oughtn't think too much, or speculate, he calls it, that she'll damage her gift for naive painting; but she thinks of some woman she paid a twelfth step call on once when she'd no business, how she'd had to push aside the mountains of old bills and supermarket flyers, canceled checks, and saucers of old food to reach the kitchen table, talk to the woman.

Was Mounty trying to reestablish the house of their childhood? She doesn't think she could have borne the travesty. No it was meant to be, perhaps, that she should have been taken off, that Fitchburg train; be here, this city with the mad people released from Metropolitan State Hospital who kissed you on the street; be here with Warren in his workshop for elderly, infirm, naïve painters…

Well, it wasn't correct to call Mike O'Sullivan a naïve painter, he was rendering, today, a pheasant whose feathers you had to touch to establish it was paint; she never in a thousand years could put each plume in place the way he does it, some lying under, some over. Would she if she could?

She might. She feels sometimes a twinge of jealousy.

But as usual her messing about today has come up with something that pleases her. Makes her giddy in fact. Her tree seems to have been assumed into the sky. The colors are not bad, either. Somehow, trusting to her instinct, colors often came right for her.

Leave it, Warren tells her. Leave it there.

You're always saying that. I leave it I have nothing else to do, two hours. Her happy time, she's jealous of anything that diminishes it, even an occasional success. But he's right, she sees, another of Henrietta's messes that comes right. Would she know it if it wasn't for Warren? Probably. But it would have been a tricky business. How it tickles her, this painting. Why did she never try it before? Here is Mike, through all his years on ships, he always knew, someday he'd paint, and Warren studying at The New School when he was fifty-four years old. Well, it was part of the general waste. It won't bear thinking, not on her painting day.

VII

Wednesday, Henrietta Rose is ill, oh nothing serious, scratchy throat and aching limbs. She waves away the van, and takes *The Boston Globe* to bed with her for a bit of self-administered Reality Orientation: Friday, November 19, A flock of storms are working their way up the coast, through Pennsylvania and the mid Atlantic to New England. Snow is expected west of Worcester. Sleet and freezing rain expected east. In Washington, the young Colombian minister of Justice announces she'll return to Bogotá, continue work of extraditing drug cartel in spite of risk to her young family's lives.

How brave, thinks Henrietta. She can never hear of bravery in others without wondering if she, Henrietta Rose, could ever equal it. What had she ever shown of bravery? Already she feels the ebb of spirits a day in bed can always cause her. She has an edifying book beside her pillow, some letters of a poet that that girl, Priscilla, who sometimes comes to the Sunshine Club with those three sisters she cares for, has pressed on her. Edifying reading can sometimes restore her. But she doesn't open it, sets aside the *Globe* and turns on her side to think about the young woman in Colombia.

This is the leaf of the coca tree; it's chewed by Indian laborers. said one of her husband's workers to her, pulling off a leaf and handing it to her once in one of those long ago quaint days: The *marijuaneros* were old men who dreamed in doorways, one or two to every town. It had been so for centuries she assumed, unchanging.

What has changed it? We, of course, in our desire for magic—our mass, our massive desire for magic—have put this young Minister of Justice and her small children in this peril...

She can recall the first inkling of this huge problem back in the days of everyone's excessive beer drinking her last year of college when she took up with Gerald and they lay on the floor of Jack Dawes' attic apartment in town and read pages of a novel Jack was writing that were strewn all over the floor, and drank straight out of beer bottles and cans—Lutie would have found it monstrous—and someone started talking about a book Aldous Huxley had written about peyote. If we could have gotten some of that we would have instantly taken it up, she thinks; but none of us knew where to get it, so we just kept drinking beer. Yes, but what interested us, she recalls, was the spiritual experience Aldous Huxley was hinting at. It seemed so superior to mere drunkenness! And see what it has led to.

She falls asleep and wakes up hour later feeling almost well and this depresses her as it takes away excuse for staying home.

Ah, Geoffrey! She remembers, lets him in to weave about her legs as she makes invalid food and breathes in steamy tea. Must indulge myself, she thinks. She admires the order of her kitchen, the health of her geraniums; they won't bloom inside, but she appreciates the thriving green, and luxurious leafing of her Swedish ivy. I am ill, and must be grateful for small pleasant things. An awful lot of things that could have happened to me, didn't, she tells herself: among them gas explosions in her romance with ending it. She could have blown up an entire apartment house full of people whom she knew. She recalls the day she turned the gas on, put a Schubert Quartet on the tape player and drank a bottle of vodka. Doesn't remember anything after that until waking in the hospital.

Yes, she will be grateful and read some more of the poet's letters in the edifying book. And she reads, there at her pleasant table, the breezy letters full of a poet's observations—You would never know their author put her head in the oven at least as often as Henrietta—this blank statement:

I take the Antabuse on weekdays.

So she can work, teach, be dependable.

A truer note. She must need the booze to write her poems, thinks Henrietta, and the Antabuse so she can work, and buy the booze. Sad. Can the poems be worth it? And are they like these mostly upbeat letters full of lovely little pictures. Hiding the banal truth of the Antabuse?

No, the poems are true and fine, and built of pain she recognizes. Truer than the letters. The price, the dreary Antabuse. Lots of poets are alcoholics, she has read. You never meet them in the basements. Are the basements death to poetry?

But Antabuse...Can anything be drearier than Antabuse? She hasn't met a poet in these basements yet, only some gifted Irish storytellers, translated from their barstools into the church basements with their eloquence quite intact. Why mightn't a poet be equally translated? Somebody ought to make a study of it.

Well, she breathes a little prayer of thanks for her translation, though not a poet, and not quite intact, she has been saved from all the things that might have befallen her, and chiefly ovens. I might have been burned beyond recognition and yet lived. My face. She does like her face; and it's an old bugaboo with her, facial disfiguration. They used to scare kids in her day with those old movies of the Thirties with their scarred faces. It must be awful not to be able to traffic with your fellows out of the certitude of appalling them.

She goes in the bathroom to brush her teeth and wash her face, examining it, and finding it acceptable, though she'd rather have been dark and leathery in old age, like lady Bexborough in *Mrs. Dalloway*, than have these pinkish freckles, thinning pinkish hair; and, always, she had wished her limbs were proportioned differently, chiefly that she was more imposing, physically. Larger. People had commented on her delicate prettiness. But she felt it didn't express her. Handsome, she'd have liked to be. Imposing.

She had felt imposing in her day: The days of her extravaganzas and certain other settings; even now, I am incurably gregarious, like a dog, can't even bear the solitude of a day in bed, she tells herself.

Carol was the one that turned out handsome. Had the Rose's looks: dark abundant hair, and olive skin, and tall.

VIII

They, both of them, were wrecks when they got off that train at last, in Seattle. But Carol took herself in hand, resumed her dancer's training, ran up hills around the bed and breakfast in the Madrona sector where they stayed. She put herself on a regimen of pulpy fruit and carrot juices at midmorning, midafternoon, and before bed; she was as faithful in this as she was in keeping doctor's appointments, enduring the chemotherapy, and swallowing the drug extracted from the yew tree.

She also kept up attending the temple. These rites she'd taken up five or so years before, after receiving instruction from a rabbi she'd met at a dance recital. Her great grandfather Rose's faith. It was very curious and unexpected, and entirely private, so Henrietta never inquired about it. While Carol was at temple, she attended her own rites in basements, which she found after a quick call to the first listing in the phone book: A.

Hi, I'm Henrietta, an alcoholic from Waltham, Massachusetts.

Hi Henrietta! came the reassuring chorus. You might be anywhere, they were the same.

And she had such hope.

Then the need for Jungian analysis occurred to Carol. She felt she was attending to her body and her spirit, but neglecting her psyche.

Precisely why you need to talk to me, thought Henrietta, but she said nothing; and during one of the rests between the treatments, they went to California.

Another train; but this time they felt like tourists, having an adventure while the essence of the carrot, and the apple, and the yew tree, went about their work. She had a month for white cells to recover, must come back then for another round.

Carol met a group of dancers there, worked out with them; and they invited her to join them in a program at a church. They interpreted the liturgy at the altar set in a huge marble circle. The dancers were of many faiths, and Carol being a Jew of the Hassidic rite fit right in. Hassids dance, Ma, like King David, Carol told her.

They took two rooms on a monthly rental in Oakland, a large house full of dancers and students of the Jung institute. Carol located a Rebbe to follow; there hadn't been a live one in Seattle; but here it was hardly strange, among the holy men on every street corner, to find a Rebbe. And of course she attended daily sessions at the Jung Institute, and wrote her dreams out in a workbook every morning, attacking the bad cells on as many fronts as they could think of. Henrietta hoped that Carol was getting out the anger she must feel. She knew from magazines and books, her recourse in every emergency, that anger unexpressed could be a cause of cancer.

She wished that she could say some things to help this on; but Carol turned it all aside: No big deal, she'd say when Henrietta brought up things like cat burials. But of course it was a big deal. I wouldn't let her cry. I never would allow it.

And was it later that she needed to die, and I wouldn't let her? No, oh no! It can't be true!

The afternoon has turned to ashes, sun setting prematurely in November. She couldn't ever, after living near the equator thirty years, readjust to New England's early winter dusks.

And Carol wanted more than anything to live...She was alive now, still, unquiet ghost, in Henrietta's mind. Oh, help me, help me someone...God. What do I want? Her death, so I can live? Her quietude I need to lay all four of their unquiet ghosts in forgetfulness. Forgetfulness, is what I wanted from the *Bwana Bap*, the *Ron de Caldas*, *aguardiente*: the people's drink, four pesos the half liter.

And at that time, they were normal, it appeared to her, healthy children, got out of scrapes all by themselves. As self-absorbed as she and Mounty in their alchemy. Why didn't they need her then, but need her now? Oh, help me!

The phone rings then. It makes her jump. She considers letting it ring itself to silence. Isn't it enough this dreadful day?

But she answers: Henrietta Rose here, in her patrician voice.

This is Debbie. Barely audible.

Who?

I'm Debbie from the Wednesday Meeting.

Henrietta hasn't an idea—her infirmity—who this is, but says, Oh, yes. What is it?

Oh, It's everything... A tiny voice from the bottom of a well.

Have you been drinking?

Yes, the tiny voice says. She'd gone to a barbeque and found herself with a glass of wine in hand before she knew it. But the trouble really started when her boyfriend made her move to a shack in woods where he kept goats. I mean, he leaves me with the goats, and there's a kid...

Goats?

And a kid I didn't know he had.

A goat!

No, a kid. And he goes off, I think he's seeing the mother of this kid.

Well, no, it must be human child, Henrietta thinks.

And now he wants me to have a baby, and I tried and lost it; now he isn't interested and I'm all alone and no hot water not a toilet even. I walked five miles to the train station.

What train station?

I don't know. It's somewhere close to Concord.

Henrietta can't imagine goats in Concord.

I thought of you. You were the speaker at the Thursday… I got on the train, and now I'm at the station in West Concord. I got off to call you and I'm getting on the next train.

When did you drink? Henrietta tells herself it doesn't matter that she can't remember this particular girl. She was simply another classic, classic dipsomaniac like herself.

Yesterday. the girl says, There were some winter campers in the woods…

But not today?

So, damn it, it is probably worth her while. They're always talking about the first drink, how important it is not to take it; but in Henrietta's experience it had been the second, not to take the second drink, had saved her, brought her back appalled at herself.

You didn't drink today, that's good. You come, then, come to me. Get off the train in Waltham. Take the bus to Lexington at the bottom of the Common. I'm only a minute's walk from Wallex Plaza. Get off there, go left. It's number thirty six, upstairs apartment. Door on right.

O.K. The voice a little stronger now.

Oh, God, oh God. What have I done? Henrietta paces round and has another cup of tea.

At four, the bell rings, and the pathetic little creature enters. Debbie. Henrietta has no remembrance. How can she remember every melting little girl who chiefly comes to meetings to complain of boyfriends?

Tell me about these goats, she says. I can't imagine goats in Concord.

Well it's in Littleton. I got a ride to Concord. I was thinking first of coming to O'Ryan's Daughter. This was the tavern on Water Street.

Oh, then it was fortunate you called me. Must she now be warm and welcoming as O'Ryan's Daughter clientele is to a drunk? Oh dear!

I've been sick… she says. She has a sudden urge to flee this scene. But we'll go out, have coffee, maybe window shop a little.

Yes! The girl lights up. Exactly what I'd like. Let the goats starve. I don't care. One got away and I couldn't catch him. Let him find them starved, or dead.

Poor little goats. She'd always had a fondness for them. But they aren't her goats, or this girl's either, Henrietta tells herself. She'll alert the animal rescue. Too many humans in trouble to get excited about goats and whales and such, is how Henrietta has always felt.

And so they go to Wallex, to the Red Rooster Coffee Shop and order breakfast at four in the afternoon. Scrambled eggs and whole wheat toast and orange marmalade. What a good idea, girl says and Henrietta starts to feel a little better.

It is spitting rain, when they get out, and so they go inside the stores, and that, of course, is what she's wanted, Debbie, all along.

Henrietta follows her about and watches in horror as the girl picks up bras and panties, slips and silky blouses, slips them in a Harris Shoe bag she unfolds from her pocketbook; and then selects a jar of face cream she demurely pays for at the checkout.

Henrietta's heart is thumping, and her face is burning when they leave, but she has to leave it in the category of goats and whales, things she can't do anything about. She does, however, tell the girl that after she's been going to meetings for a while she probably won't want to do this anymore.

It's six o'clock when they get back, and she's exhausted and must go to bed. She lets the girl sleep on the couch in the sitting room.

VIV

Next morning she's forgotten why she has this guest and tries in vain to reconstruct. Finally, turning to her datebook, she sees

Tom at Ten

And decides to turn herself and this new burden over to him. After all, he's got now: Fourteen days and seven hours, fifteen minutes, as he announces soon as he sees her, can take up a burden or two—too late she's recalled the edict about never doing twelfth steps by yourself.

.   And so they crowd into his cab and whirl down to the Italian Church and she turns the girl loose into the room, and mixes herself a cup of chocolate, and listens to Jean Paul tell about his wife who joined that terrorist organization, Alanon, and how he didn't come into these halls because he saw the light, but rather because he felt the heat.

She starts to feel a little better. In fact forgets the girl entirely. Who? she asks when Tom inquires about this girl before dropping her at Sunshine Club. She's after all a handicapped, and elderly...the Korsakoff's etcetera.

Applecake, says Adie Blakey at the Sunshine Club. Pudding pie! She used to be the only Blakey; now her sister Winnie, who says: Obfuscation in a bullfrog voice, has joined them, and another sister, Megan, who says:

...chloroform them both, I thought I'd get away with it...

Objurgation, rejoins Winnie. And Alfred starts to pull his pants down. No, that isn't appropriate here, Alfred, calls Rebecca, going to him, and offering a chocolate.

I had a single child, Megan Blakey, who seems sensible enough, says to Henrietta, who is mixing instant mashed for lunch. And there wasn't any Pill then.

Yes, says Henrietta. I had four. I remember I could get The Pill in pharmacies where I lived. You only had only to say your periods were irregular. And the native women hadn't a clue. They used to douche with aspirin water, jump up and down on the bed when they'd had intercourse.

Coitus interruptus, that's what, Megan Blakey says...

Oh, yes, well... humphs Henrietta in her patrician voice.

Not a thing they'd teach you at Holy Cross or Boston College, how to have a single brat, goes on Megan.

Well, I was glad I had the others, Henrietta says.

Was she? Was ever a word she said the truth? Wouldn't she have been better without? She could be happy now.

Did it make you happy, that one child? she asks.

She did until we found she hadn't any music. Music was everything to us, I and my Louis. It was a holy thing...Every concert precious. We heard the greats: Charles Munch, and Rudolf Serkin...

Henrietta notes the pile of *Opera News* in her lap.

But your daughter, she's a comfort to you now...

Oh, no. She lives in California. I haven't seen her twenty years. She sends a card at Mother's Day and such. Big as a tea tray, must cost five dollars at least. You'd think with both of us musical...Louie played the oboe in one of Roosevelt's Depression orchestras. You'd think she might inherit, wouldn't you? Well, there are always consolations.

Are there?

Oh, yes. There was my Louis, there was music, still, and books.

You read these magazines? Henrietta's noted they are dated in the Fifties.

Well, my eyesight's gone. Priscilla comes. She's always come, the evenings. I live for evenings. A life of Mozart, we are reading. We've read it several times. And these magazines. I bring them with me here to keep them out of the hands of that Fahey woman who comes sometimes to care for my sisters. She would throw them out as soon as breathe.

No wickeder race exists than the Irish. Take my word. And that woman's worse than the worst of them. "No Irish need apply." They had that right!

But you...are, aren't you?

I've expunged it from my person.

Objurgation, says one of the sisters, the severe one, who looks like Megan.

Apple cake, says the other one, in the chair.

My Louie was an orphan, raised up by Shakers. They didn't approve of sex and reproduction and are dying out, you know.

Ah, really? Henrietta is impressed, though horrified. First sensible conversation she's ever had in this place. Well almost sensible.

They hoped, originally, the orphans that they raised would carry on. Of course, they didn't. A mistake. But in the main I think it's wisdom to assure your...your demise, well don't you think? It's what the benighted Irish ought to do, and they would except for priests' interference. My daughter's avoided reproduction, so I've done my part.

Had cerebrovascular accidents, three of us; only I had sense to fight. I told them fight; but neither would. I'd have drunk cyanide if I'd...

Well, so would all of us, says Henrietta, looking into the glittering pitiless eyes of her companion. Well, some of us.

X

Tuesday Paint!

Her favorite day.

She starts her next painting: House in West Boylston, of course, with a wall removed. The attic wall.

What's that flying out the window? Mike wants to know.

Envelopes. She says. We were entering contests.

Contests?

Find the hidden bunny. Finish the riddle. Mounty was sure we would win if we entered enough.

After the alchemical messes and the investigation of falling bodies that followed, Henrietta turned to her mud houses and her dreams of horses; and Mounty turned to contests in the newspapers and magazines. It brought them back together briefly, for she had to participate of course; it increased the odds. In fact, Mounty even invented a third sibling, who entered the contests as Benno Pierce. Henrietta was valuable as she was as clever as Mounty at writing jingles and answering riddles and finding hidden cats and owls and bunnies in forest scenes.

They never won; it flummoxed Mounty. Must be the mail, the kids live closer, judges get their answers first. He spent his money on special delivery sometimes, and nothing. Just a matter of keeping up. Statistically we have to win sometime. The odds...

And that was where he ended up. A statistician. He studied the subject, that is, in college. Then he worked for firms that played the market, bonds she thinks it was.

She doesn't know what happened after that. She lost him somewhere, up there in the attic, during the puzzles sometime. She never shared his anxiety to win the way she shared the messes with him and the leaping out of trees. What did they need money, prizes, for? They had as many bicycles and electric toys as any child could want. What would they have done with money anyhow? She will have to leave him for now as a smudgy figure up there in the dark. She cannot think where Mounty might have saved himself...where she...How careless she had been, and stupid.

Mounty won a scholarship to the London School of Economics, and married there, another student: Lovely girl from Cornwall. A redhead; and they'd had a pretty daughter with a head full of copper ringlets, who'd been a toddler at the time of Henrietta's wedding. Had they left him, or he, them?

Beautiful children. Her own young family: how beautiful they'd been; all of them, not just Carol. There, she might have stuck. Had they been undone, she and Mounty, by Lutie's evanescences? They might equally have been held fast by Nummie's strong presence in the kitchen.

She must ask him. She must see him. She'd consulted enough doctors over the years with these questions. Why had she never thought to ask her brother? Instead of bothering him about his drinking, which got them nowhere, she might have inquired with him where this closing in process, this letting go of spouses and children, had begun with each of them.

Flying out of the attic she paints a row of envelopes addressed to contests. She wonders how could they have been so intent, so organized, as children; and so careless as adults.

She wakes to snow next morning. Lies in bed listening to plows. By the time she's up to investigate, she's missed the van,

She and Mounty always hoped for types of weather seldom came to Worchester County, Massachusetts—being too easterly for tornadoes, too westerly for hurricanes. But snow brought with it possibilities; and even now, in her sixties, it could awake that fervent watching, holding down the temperature, that liked to climb and turn it all to mush, with her will; and holding back the winds that caused it to pass too rapidly, so it dumped its load in hated New Hampshire.

She remembers wintery day, when she and Gerald were living in an apartment house in Philadelphia, they had one storm that closed down the city. They woke up to feel their ceiling thumping; the couple lived above them jubilant, jumping up and down on the bed and shouting: Don't have to go to work today!

It's crazy. In some senses, one never does grow up. She watches it filling in between the blades of grass, then overcoming heat of sidewalks, streets, to start to cover between the passing, cars, and, finally, by the time they line up for the van, it's won; and they make footprints trailing out, and ride muffled, slithering through it.

In Philadelphia, Gerald worked at Merck and had to take some extra courses in pharmacology at Temple. It was then he brought those books home she read from cover to cover, diagnosing herself in a 1955 Merck manual; and, later, when they went to South America, practicing pharmacology on herself. No wonder her children came out funny.

She walked around the streets alone at night in Philadelphia, feeling an exquisite loneliness. But why? She had a new husband came home every night slept with her on the double mattress on the floor. They didn't buy any other furniture. They ate sitting on the bed from tray tables someone gave them for their wedding. Gerald wouldn't buy anything, sure he'd be drafted any minute for the Korean war.

She'd get up from that mattress in the night and walk, walk all over the neighborhood. They lived then near the Loyola campus, north Philly; after fleeing the heat of Spruce Street, downtown. As she recalled it she was looking for someone to talk to. Why didn't she talk to Gerald? She loved him. She was crazy for him that last year of college for both of them; that spring she lay with him under hedges, giving him her body, risking expulsion; it was the fifties, after all. Risking flunking.

She was crazy. Gerald at least studied for his tests. He wasn't about to jeopardize his four point eight average for any girl. And, after they were married, he slept like an infant, never knew a thing about her midnight walks, her nights of reading his textbooks—she could have passed any of his exams then, she believed. He never let a thing keep him up past nine or ten, so he could get to work, fresh as a new laid egg.

No, Gerald was serious about life. His mother loved him utterly; and, he satisfied his father easily with his studious habits. Then she, Henrietta, came along to give him her body. He was completely satisfied.

And then his company was come into his life to hold out goodies; all he needed was to stay out of the army, and see he got good food to eat, and rest, and put his foot firmly on the rungs of corporate advancement...

What was she looking for in those textbooks? To find out what was the matter with her. Something was the matter, and there must be a remedy, some chemical, some alchemy. And the boy she married? The boy she called The Alchemist? She threatened his composure from the first, her sleeping late, her failure to buy food at times, her desire to stay out late at parties; but he simply moved them to places where servants could be hired to supply her lacks. It came to where she needn't even get up in the morning, look after the children; there was money to hire help for every area she failed in. His feet were firmly moving up the rungs.

Except as hostess. There she shone. It might have stumped him had she failed him there.

The sun comes out in the afternoon and nearly melts all the five inches they'd worked so hard to push aside that morning. To make up for her sloth, Henrietta walks to the Old Timer's Meeting in the VFW just down the street.

Lloyd M. is speaking. Lloyd is eighty, sober forty. Used to work at the Mill.

Hey Lloyd, you got new sneakers. Watch it, kid could murder you for them sneakers, says a wise guy.

Lloyd clears his throat, looks down approvingly at his sneakers:

I'm Lloyd, an alcoholic. I figured other day I've said that maybe one hundred twenty thousand times. I bought these running shoes myself, not used to it since Ruthie died. She probably wouldn't have chosen them. I didn't care when I was drinking, what she thought or didn't think. Or anybody else, except the guy sitting on the barstool next to me; I worried if he liked me, never mind the ones at home who loved me.

Oh, it's true, thinks Henrietta.

It's an oldtimers' meeting, but most of them today are young. She puts her hand up to speak:

I'm Henrietta, an alcoholic. I try not to forgot to say it. I forget a lot. The Korsakoff's. You young people want to see a reason not to drink, well look at me. I have to write down who I am in a notebook every night so I can wake up in the morning and remember. Laughter.

That's all I've got to say. Had something else, but I forget... More laughter.

Lucy M., who's sitting on her right has just come back from burying her son-in-law; she puts her hand up: This group of typical piggish, infantile drunks— that's what we are, you know—managed to put a meeting on in Terre Haute, Indiana, that was just like here, she says. Identical. To comfort me after the funeral. No, I'm joking. It was their regular kind of meeting. And it occurred to me what a miracle that was; you talk to anyone, it happens everywhere. You'd think there was some great quality control inspector going around checking up on them on them, to keep them up to snuff...ha ha!

But there is no one, no one's in charge; and there was even someone in that room in Terre Haute that was drunk and people only said to him, "Keep coming," and went on with it.

A miracle, and we never notice it.

Yes, Amen, says someone.

They stand for the Our Father, and Lloyd's hand on her left is hard and dry and swallows hers up, and Lucy's on her right is soft and warm, like holding a small bird.

It's was true, she says to Lucy after. What you said about...about...

The meeting in Terre Haute?

Yes. I went to meetings everywhere when I was with my daughter, and she was dancing in churches, writing down her dreams for the Jung Institute, and we were dragging ourselves to Seattle, and then to San Francisco, then Seattle again, and this experimental medicine, and that yoga exercise, and the running and the deep breathing. And all the time she's dying.

Yes, oh, yes. The tears come in Lucy's eyes; she touches Henrietta's hand before they wrap their scarves about them and she follows Tom out to his truck.

XI

They visualized together, white corpuscles reproducing, juices, grains and yoghurt nourishing, the muscle tone returning; Carol would be flushed some days, after the dancing sessions, or the run around the little park their rooms on Tamarindo Street looked over.

Was it fever? Henrietta couldn't bear to think this; but the day before they flew back to Seattle, sometime in the middle of December, Carol said it out: I've had a fever. The nutritionist she was seeing at the Women's Collective advised her to fast, drink water only, so the next day, packing, getting out to airport, she drank water only. She was so weak when they arrived at the clinic five hours later, they hospitalized her.

She was there through Christmas, an awful time; but then they got her blood count up, and started the vincristine, so they could feel again that they were fighting; the vincristine was battling, and the emaciation and the vomiting were due to Carol's body being a battleground. A battle was being waged not lost, not lost.

And after New Year's they declared there had to be another pause in the hostilities, advised a quiet place; and one, thought Henrietta, that didn't cost so much. And Carol, noting fall in peso, and having in her folders of information details of a clinic, decided the time had come to try it, Mexico.

So she wouldn't forget what people sometimes said in meetings, Henrietta Rose sometimes tried to write down things in a notebook. It was very boring and troublesome, making her impatient, so she'd done it in a kind of shorthand, and now, this morning, Monday, looks at it, can barely make out...Lucy...Oldtimers meeting, French Church...hand like...warm bird...Terre Haute...son-in-law... Carol...tell her...touches me.

She sits at kitchen table with a second cup of tea, and in a second notebook that she'd saved for something, puts it back together in her best literary manner gained from reading all those books from Lutie's shelves, the Harvard Classics. Reading over what she'd written, she finds herself moved as if someone else had written it. A novel sensation, like her first painting. So she leaves the good notebook on the table, puts the shorthand one in the pocket book she carries daily

Interesting, how the words she'd scrawled brought back other words. An exercise like the ones she does now, holding on to the kitchen sink to stretch her calves and bring her heels down.

Oh, but what's the use? Well, if she could hold the present. If the recent memories her brain erases—like a reel before it's hardly recorded—could be forcibly, like this, retained, and fill this vacuum, then the painful past would not rush in so, filling all the space she needs to carry on her present happy life.

At the Sunshine Club they're sitting round the table where they do crafts, and Isa Babcock tells the story about the time she was invited to a wedding in western Massachusetts, and, walking from the station at Northhampton, lost her brooch.

The stone fell out right on the road. I saw it glittering there; and so I took a shortcut through the pine woods and took the smallest bead of pitchpine on my finger, and with it fastened back the stone, it was a topaz.

You told that story twenty times, says Bertha, who if she mightn't have all her marbles, could remember like an elephant.

And Henrietta, who doesn't recall ever hearing it, notes it in her notebook.

I've always heard that a topaz was bad luck, says Megan, who's been forced to sit with them; if she had her choice, she'd wheel herself away from everybody. But she does refuse to cut out shapes of bells and candy canes to paste in the windows.

Oh no, that's only an old tale, says Isa. Topaz are the loveliest stone, like smoke that's captured.

Henrietta takes her notebook out and jots this down. Megan sniffs and closes her eyes and puts her headphones on in spite of being forbidden.

Megan reminds Henrietta of a boy they used to send round to various churches and Sunday schools with her and Mounty. Harry and Lutie'd given up on churching themselves, but felt, however, along with this boy's parents— Charles Galkin was his name—that children ought to be exposed to various faiths, at least the more respectable ones.

They were to sample each, then choose. Well Charles Galkin wasn't having any of it. She remembers sitting in the Baptist Sunday school basement, smelling of coal furnace and old hymn books, noting he wouldn't recite with them, kept his mouth in severe line like Megan's, even though he certainly could read as well as any of them, ended being sent to University of Chicago when the rest of them were just entering high school.

No, as to churches, she and Mounty never chose.

Though she, at least, enjoyed it, especially the singing; so she did the same as Lutie when it came to her own children, with the same results, though Carol was an exception.

Not of course until adulthood. What did Carol think of this method of religious upbringing, she asked when they sat in the clinic in Seattle the second time.

Well when we went to Mass was what I most remember, Carol said. You went with us.

Yes, I thought it brought us closer to the culture of where we lived. I was fed up with the company types we were supposed to hang around with. The Best Foods Family, they called it, and they all belonged to the Country Club and to the Episcopal Church in Santa Rita, and never noticed even they were in a foreign country. People came barefoot to that little church we went to, and their shirttails hanging out...

Yes, I liked that, Henrietta goes on. It was our parish, our parish church. In spite of that big house we lived in, in Maranon, I think it was, the neighborhood was poor, a part of it—there wasn't any zoning there, and you could live in a mansion and have a lot of shacks around you. I liked to think that God was in that church in spite of the priest who struck me as rather ignorant. I liked it not trailing around after famous preachers like the Protestants I know who're always searching for a church that suits them, where the sermons and the choir are worthy of their taste and intelligence.

Yes, Carol said. You almost convinced me, though the other kids all laughed at you, kneeling and crossing yourself backwards.

Did I really. Isn't it supposed to invite the Devil or something? Heavens!

And once we were about to take the Host, and some old woman tapped me on the shoulder and told me not to swallow it; she'd seen us buy and ice cream in the Plaza on the way.

Oh, Lord!

So, well, I put it off, and never thought about religion till I was in college, and then it was as literature, Carol told her. I didn't have a lot of time to read the Bible and such things until I graduated, then I went back and finished things like Thomas Mann's *Joseph and his Brothers*, and I read the Old Testament, right through, as if it was a novel. And didn't understand the half, it's why I went to Rabbis later, got some help. But at first it was different. It was literature.

I see. It was vaguely satisfying to skirt religion in their talk, in case the vincristine, the cortex of the yew should fail them. Religion was supposed to be comforting. She didn't believe it at the time.

In case the vincristine and the yew should fail them.

She could only rest her mind on this possibility a fraction of a moment.

It's why what happened to me when Owen was born is so strange, she remembers Carol saying.

What's strange? You never told me.

Well, I always kept it to myself. I thought it might lose...its power for me, Carol had said.

And I wasn't a fit person to tell, back then, thinks Henrietta. Carol was dozing off all through this conversation. She spent the major part of those days in a light sleep while Henrietta watched the pinkish fluid flow through the tube.

Henrietta herself had started going to services in the Congregational Church a few years back, after years of speculations, as she was sitting in their basements, about the rites performed above them in the sanctuary, and their relation to the rites below.

She actually goes quite regularly now, upstairs to join the dying remnant of a Congregational body of thirty souls in the big white church downtown. She used to think they worried mostly about their silverware.

For not only was their basement filled with drunks, their chapel, built in some never forgotten heyday of the silver service, was filled with Haitian and Hispanic Pentecostal ranters.

I thought, since you go down there...that is I see you go down there to the kitchen... This is how she was accosted a couple Sundays ago by one of the Misses Petersham:

Yes, I make the coffee for an organization, Henrietta answered cagily.

We wondered if you might perhaps have seen a silver ladle to a punchbowl that we're missing.

Well you might perhaps have said good morning first, Henrietta'd said, thinking to bring a little lesson in Christian behavior from the folks in the basement.

But now she's sorry she said it. She's developed a theory that it's in the nature of the faith to bubble up from basements and rented chapels and flow into the old sanctuaries. And she can admit the importance of the folks in the sanctuaries, for they conserve—along with the silver service—the lovely symbols, stories, lovely words that are subsumed, below, into the barely serviceable "Higher Power" in order to serve them up to drunks who happen to be atheists and agnostics or followers of the Tao or God knows what.

7pm Baptist Ch. Speak

Her datebook says. It's walking distance and she traverses the two blocks with just one cane.

There's one speaker before her, a young girl who tells about drinking tequila sunrises and listening to Linda Ronstadt and calling up old boyfriends. There's been a beans and franks supper for the homeless, earlier so the back rows are filled with their belching presence and she's scarcely begun speaking when the one that's known as The Professor lifts up his head and mumbles:

I love you Henrietta.

She's used to this, and merely pulls the mike closer to talk over him. She used to see him sober, had a couple conversations with him; she is, as she knows herself, inveterate practitioner of social skills, and so she gets into trouble sometimes like this.

Love you! The voice is stronger now he's digested his bellyful of beans.

Keep coming, someone at the back says.

She never thinks what she will say before she speaks—she wouldn't remember, any case—but takes her cue from the speaker before her, remembering the Linda Ronstadt.

I listened to music too, she says, while I was drinking. But it was Brahms I listened to...

Adore you, Henrietta!

...and SAUL BELLOW I WANTED TO CALL UP. I HAD A GIRLFRIEND ONCE WHO ACTUALLY DID THAT, CALLED HIM UP AND TOLD HIM THAT SHE LOVED HIM, loved his books that is. She wasn't even drunk. But I couldn't do it, even drunk. I mean to say, however, that a person doesn't only drink to drown his sorrows, but to make good moments better...

Darling Lady!

...MAKE THE NICE A LITTLE NICER. She wonders, in her vanity, what it is he fancies about her, face or figure. Habit nearly killed me. Once I put a favorite tape on—a string quartet I used to like—and turned the oven on and drank a pint of vodka. I turned the oven pilot off but forgot the burner pilots. I might have blown up an apartment full of people...

Fairest one! Someone's brought him a cup of coffee and his head is slumped now on a table. Hopefully he'll sleep.

I didn't need the vodka, turns out. Music is its own pleasure. Everything is its own pleasure.

A beautiful soul! He raises his head in tribute, before finally slumping on to the table. Ah, well, she thinks. I might have known it wasn't my face.

XII

They flew when they left Seattle the second time. Carol's weakness wouldn't allow another train trip. And Henrietta found herself in another cement block airport, after thirty years, with urchins crowding round her: *Una moneda, Doña. Dios te bendiga!*

And she knew there wouldn't be any dancing at the altar where they had arrived, or women's collectives, that she was all the spiritual resource there would be. She found a meeting:

Soy Henrietta, soy una alcólica.

They met in a community center in a dusty square behind the church. She walked there during Carol's morning treatment. She was the only woman, and she tickled them immensely. They called her *La Companerita.*

The substance they treated Carol with here came from the pits of apricots. It wasn't any more far fetched than something extracted from the cortex of the yew tree was it?

Reminds her of the Alchemy.

While Mounty involved himself with the physics of falling bodies, she moved out of the attic into the garden, involved herself with cooking pots of acorns, bark and next year's willow buds stripped off, in a medium of rainwater mixed with mud. But she remembers something of lassitude about these last mixings, as if she were losing faith a few years behind Mounty. We can feed it to our dolls, remarked her insipid cousin, Nancy, that Lutie used to bring to play.

No it's a medicine, she'd inform this creature. We are doctors.

Oh, the girl said. She was very pretty; but not bright, and Henrietta hated her.

She doesn't remember whether it was she or Mounty made the discovery of mud, not as medium but as building material. She seems to recall herself alone constructing shelters for turtles out of sticks and mud daub, just like those later shacks in Sogamoso, and still later there in Mexicali. She plotted ever larger shelters, for a dog, a horse. She dreamed of horses, sitting on the bough of the misshapen oak she'd fitted out with halter and blanket. She knew that Lutie'd never admit a flesh and blood horse, even though they had a pasture, so dreamed a clockwork beast inside something like the horsehair rug that made an island in their nursery. And she sat up very high on this horse and he was like a real horse in every way, except he didn't eat or make manure to bother Lutie. Anything was possible to their science she and Mounty thought until they lost that faith.

It was in a clinic something like this that you were born, she said to Carol one day in Mexicali when Carol's health was a little improved. They didn't worry here about corpuscles, and simply leaving them alone seemed to restore a little strength to her, so they were sitting in a little lounge with leatherette seats opposite a family whose aged mother had brought a supper for everyone including the patient in a set of stackable aluminum pans. The clinic overlooked the little city's red tile roofs, and you could hear the roosters crowing, and see the kites shaped like buzzards flying from a naked hill the other side of town.

I hoped you'd tell me what you started to, back in Seattle, about Owen's birth. Henrietta said.

Oh, well you know. You hope for a child without results for even a few months, you start to feel like those women, Sarah, Rachael, and then, I told you, I'd read the Old Testament. As literature.

Yes.

Well it was a year for us trying to get pregnant. I think that had something to do with it.

Of course. I always thought you used something.

Oh, everybody thought that. I didn't fret about it every moment. But the worry was there. I took my temperature. I stood on my head, practically, after every time we did it. An old story, many have it worse.

But what? You do want to tell me? If you don't...

Oh, yes. Of course.

I'd earned it, Henrietta thinks now. If ever I could have earned it, I'd earned it then.

Well, that was the background. I think it comes in somehow. And then I did...conceive, Carol took up the story.

Ah, yes.

It was the most tremendous thing to me. I was a little hysterical, I'm sure. And I went nine months sure that something would happen and I'd lose him; but nothing happened; until the night he was born, not breathing...

But he was, all right.

Oh, yes. It was a matter of five minutes panic, nothing like the year I waited, nothing; if it weren't for my state of mind.

Of course.

So, they put me in my room, and let him stay beside me, to calm me; and I held his little hand, and didn't sleep at all for fear that he'd stop breathing.

I didn't sleep. And yet I had a dream. There was a cracked pane in the window of the room and I kept looking at it, to assure myself I wasn't sleeping...

A dream. A waking dream, I think of it. And I was Hannah...

Hannah?

In the Bible. She prayed for a child and one was given to her. Samuel. I didn't see her I was her.

But she must give him back. That was the significant part. She must give him back to God...well to the temple. So she did, and he heard voices, heard God's voice when he was still a child...

Owen Samuel, you called him. Owen after his grandfather, the Samuel mystified all of us.

Of course. It was hidden in his name, a secret, so I wouldn't forget. No danger of that these last few years.

But he's fine. A little troubled adolescence.

Mom, he isn't fine. He hears voices and they aren't God's. Jason promised he'd see a doctor but he hasn't, I just know..

But...

When Jason left me, Owen got into grass, I guess. Some other stuff.

Of course, it's in the family...

Schizophrenia?

Of course not! Alcohol, addiction. It's the same...

The doctor he saw called it schizophrenia.

But I heard voices in my drink. A lot of us did. I don't believe it. We'll get him help; he mustn't touch the drugs.

But Carol wasn't listening. He hears voices. God's little joke, for thinking it was literature. I told the Rebbe about it, until now the only person. And he told me some hard things, you can't imagine how difficult...

Well what?

To give him. Like Hannah, to give him back. I do, I try. I thought this waking dream some kind of blessing, a gift...but it's a curse!

No, no, my darling. In my meetings, we do that, we give people to the Higher Power. We think they've a Higher Power just as we have!

Oh, your meetings!

No, no, don't mock it. It was literature, remember, brought you to your waking dream. He, God, can use the oddest means, you see. I see salvation every meeting that I go to. No, don't mock it. Just keep doing what that Rebbe told you, in your mind. I do it for your brother, Charles. I can hardly bear to see him, but I hold him in my mind. I see him whole.

But how can I? I'm conjuring armies waging battles against cancer cells.

Well, that's just why! You give him. Give him over, then you're free to fight your battle.

Yes. Carol took a couple deep breaths and leaned back in the leatherette settee and closed her eyes: You think a lot, then, about Charles?

Oh, yes.

I never knew that. I used to think, when he was living with us for that year or so, that I was the only one that cared. I guess we don't know much what other people are thinking, do we. And we hardly ever tell each other.

Carol sat forward suddenly. It's too hard. It's like I wanted that child too much, and so I got what I wanted and then it's pay pay pay! And now I'm tired. Maybe I don't want to live.

Henrietta didn't know what to say. A battle was being waged she had no power to turn. It is like that with almost every mother, she said. Even though they aren't given visions. That's why the old stories have so much power. They are everybody's. Everybody's child is special.

When she has the strength, she phones Jason, asks about her grandson, and listens with impatience to psychiatrist's reports about fixations on the mother and abandonment issues.

Such a waste of time, though she must remember all the time she wasted on various therapists. Does he drink? she asks, is told the drinking was only symptom of a blah blah blah. She can't listen.

Of course, it was in the family. Lutie was a scandal on a grand scale, in spite of being such a lady, and there were tales of two great uncles ended up in madhouses. They kept Lutie going by periodically sending her for "rests." and she'd return to family seeming like someone who's been rescued from some harrowing brush with they didn't know what, but who now was "fine," a convalescent; she'd spend most of day sitting up in bed with pretty bed jackets on, and the children could each spend a half an hour with her being read to or allowed to look at her jewelry boxes, or her photograph albums; and she would once again sit at the table opposite their father, and make her witty observations about people they knew, and laugh in her ladylike way behind her napkin, and serve up the plates as they were brought in by Hulda Engbretsen, and the dessert, which was always something special because Lutie was back.

And these intervals were fairly long; and there'd be nothing to alarm until one day they'd catch a glimpse of her up-turned pumps, and hitched up skirt in the marble hallway, or beside the parental bed, or at the foot of stair, before being locked up in the nursery while Lutie was packed up and sent away again "to rest."

She and Mounty didn't play with other children, had no way of knowing every family wasn't just like theirs… Well, there were intimations, yes, there were The Bears.

They were a German family; the mother worked for them sometimes. They lived nearby on a small farm. Behr was actually the name. To Henrietta there was something bearlike about them, so they were The Bears, to her. Mama Bear was always in the kitchen: theirs, where she sometimes helped Hulda Enbretsen, or in her own, where she made substantial but economical soups, baked bread and rolls, for her large family of five girls. Their house was just across some fields, so she and Mounty visited often. It was a shabby farmhouse with a number of mostly unused outbuildings. Papa Bear had left off farming, worked now as a carpenter and odd jobs man.

He was a worn and mild man, essentially foreign. Unlike her father, he was seldom absent from home; his workshop was in a shed behind the house, and he came often into the house, and smiled at her and Mounty as if they'd only just been introduced, and treated Mrs. Bear with an old world courtliness. His English was far more broken than his wife's, perhaps because she went out to work far more than he did.

To Henrietta they were like a family in a fairy tale, and Norma Bear, the closest of the sisters to her age, was the most favored child she ever knew. Norma had an entire barn to play in. It was hers, a sturdy, empty building which she'd divided into rooms by piling up some wooden crates her father gave her, making walls with many cubbyholes to store her dolls in. She was the youngest, and most promising, child, with a marked talent for drawing. Lutie paid her once to make a pencil portrait of Mounty from a photo taken when he was five.

She thinks it must have been during Lutie's "rests" that she went to stay with them for an extended time. There were other times too, but not as long. Time went by, during these stays with a kind of measured ceremony, as if she'd been an enchanted princess. She sat on an encyclopedia during the many courses of the rather formal meals, with Papa Bear officiating, seeing that the heavy platters moved up and down the table, that their little visitor had her share, treating her with the same courtliness he treated Mama Bear; until the moment she and Norma could be excused, and return to their family of dolls, to their pretend. It was the only time she ever played with dolls. Unlike her outlaw play with Mounty, this play had an air of propriety.

It couldn't have been entirely as she remembers, she tells herself; but that didn't matter to their influence on her. And where was Mounty during Lutie's rests? Her memory is entirely dark. She guesses he was kept home with their father and Hulda Engbretsen. Was this owing to their outlaw pursuits? Did they think with Lutie absent they weren't adequately supervised. She can't recall a single instance of Lutie's supervision. It was Inez, the daily help from the Canary Islands, whose nose directed her at last to the laboratory in the third floor, who threw out the roiling crocks before they could be finally transmuted…*Huele*, oof!

But Lutie wasn't to be entirely blamed; for Henrietta from her babyhood had hidden from her, kept secret from her every scrape or bruise, or social snub. For Lutie, at the start at least, had been aggressive, prying everywhere.

When had that changed? Henrietta can recall a bath, once, Lutie leaning over the tub, and she, very young, still needing help with a bath, had said to her mother, I don't understand what the father has to do with it.

With? What? Lutie had asked.

With what the children look like. You're always telling us that Mounty looks like you and I like Daddy.

Poor Lutie. They hadn't even gotten past the question of the route of birth by then, not even past the baby terms. Her wee wee was still her wee wee, not "vagina" as it was to become momentarily, such an ugly word. And Mounty still had a wee wee, not a penis. And all of a sudden, during that bath, these new ugly words were brought out: and, worse, she was told about the monstrous function of penises, to be stuck into vaginas so that babies could resemble fathers.

Shock. To her of course, but Lutie, oh poor Lutie! Henrietta was a monster of a child!

One other conversation, only, she remembers, and also in the bath. How it came up, she can't remember; but the subject had been Ludwig Beethoven and his deafness—perhaps Lutie trying to set a higher tone after the conversation about the penises. The gist of it had been the fact that Beethoven went on writing music even when he couldn't hear any more, and that therefore she, Henrietta must take a lesson from this and not be weakened by misfortune.

Lutie, in her soft dresses at the piano, gave off a contrary message. She launched tantalizingly into various sonatas and rhapsodies she'd learned up to the hard parts, stopping in the middle of a phrase of Brahms or Beethoven. When Henrietta's time for lessons came, she made a point of learning the hard parts first.

She hardened against Lutie, probably from the time she was allowed to bathe alone, for she can't remember another intimate exchange. Poor Lutie. It wasn't her fault.

With Mounty it was different. He was friends with Lutie all his life, tender to her. It was Mounty she embraced and wept over when she went away, returned. She brazenly interfered with him, she picked the suitable children he might play with, endlessly discussed his talents, the ones he must develop publicly, the ones he might indulge in his spare time.

Her father was a courtly man, like Mr. Bear, his courtliness, however, tinged with irony. As if he played a part in one of those drawing room plays she saw in Boston as a child. She didn't pick up the irony when she was younger, but took it for benignity, and didn't harden against him.

It wasn't necessary. Unlike Lutie, he wasn't likely to lift the lid of that hermetic pot where she and Mounty roiled and fermented, sublimated into the adults they played at being.

She, for her part, modeled herself on The Bears. Why did she have four children? In emulation of Mrs. Bear, she guesses. She even strove for bearlike shabby comfort in the houses that they lived in. There must have been forty at least. Another story. Gerald waited till she was drunk, and tossed out armchairs, tables, stacks of magazines, broken lamps, and broken shoes.

But it was an emulation of an outer bearlike quality. The inner she could never grasp. The daughter of Lutie and Franklin Pierce Montegue was a fraudulent person, as her children knew.

But now? Who is she now?

I'm Henrietta. I'm an alcoholic.

She speaks the incantatory words in the crowded Bingo Hall which used to be St. Mary's School for Girls. I didn't plan to be an alcoholic when I grew up. I planned to be a chemist, if I remember rightly. Well, I married a chemist.

He used to work in an *ingenio*—that's a place where they process sugar cane. They made everything from cakes of raw sugar to *Ron de Caldas*. That was the rum I drank. They also made a kind of vodka—*aguardiente*—out of cane, as well as a purgative for cattle, and impotable alcohol—witch hazel, we call it. And they put it all in bottles of an identical shape and with a label that had a green cross on it. I remember once we were at a party, the hacienda of some friends, and they kept all these bottles on a kitchen shelf together—the ones for the cattle, the ones for the people—and someone took the wrong one down. I think it was the impotable, because the cattle purgative did look different when you poured it... But, in any case, they served it up in these fat little glasses they had for aguardiente, which is a drink you swig down all at once, then make a face, then suck a lemon slice to get rid of the awful taste; so that is what we all did, toss it down.

Well, it was the impotable, and we all lay about all afternoon in hammocks waiting to die. One young man, I remember, sang a requiem mass right through, in Latin. Yes, I won't forget that afternoon. Some of us threw up, but all survived.

So, it was her family's fault that Owen is what he is today, and in the hands of doctors. But still it made her very angry, the implication that the "abandonment issue" Jason always brought up, was Carol's fault, when it was Jason who had left her after her cancerous ovary was removed. Of course Carol then had up and died and left them all, and maybe that was what he meant.

XIII

Someone ought to be supervising you. Is Warren's comment when she tells him how she bought the seven vending machines for Charles to stock and, hopefully, collect enough to live off. I had this twenty thousand dollars when Gerald died, and meant to use it to set him up. I didn't touch the principal that paid my dividends.

Ah well, you thought you'd give it to the Mafia. says Warren

A friend of mine suggested they might be Mafiosi; and I suspected something when they drove up to my two room flat in a great limousine got stuck in the drive. But they were Jews I think.

Didn't never hear of Bugsie Seigel, did you? Mike says.

As I said, she ought to be supervised.

Well, says Mike, I guess to be one of those naive painters, you gotta be a little bit...

Naive, ah yes! she laughs. And we were supposed to order candy bars and such from them, and suddenly they disappeared, the phone was disconnected and the mail, there was no forwarding.

Of course.

And then, after the vandalism, and the spending more than we were taking in, we couldn't even put them out to the trash. I had to pay another pretty sum to haul them off, and then I heard the man I hired simply threw them in the Charles River.

Price you pay for being a naive painter.

But where was your husband all this time? Warren asks.

Dead. It was after he died.

Well, your brother then?

She excuses chauvinism of this type in Warren. He is kind under his bluster, and cares about her. And he's of her generation, when the women exacted what the men would give.

My Gerald was dead by then, and I had squandered, considerably, what he left me. And you don't know my brother.

And it was good for me. I learned a lesson.

You learned about the Bugsie Siegels. Mike says.

She laughs, her hostess laugh, but Warren's looking at her grimly.

And made myself eligible for such things as my subsidized apartment, and the Sunshine Club, and these painting classes. We'd have never met.

You could have gone to some fancy art school, like my big shot daughter.

Oh, I could have done...a thousand things... She does a Julie Andrews turn. Low as she sinks in her explorations in the subsidized life of aged, poor, infirm, the hostess in her will remain.

And how could I then be Waltham's foremost naive painter?

You know, you know... He can't help laughing. This is a joke, on me as well as you...you know what's going to happen to these canvases we're sweating over...?

Oh, I don't sweat, she tinkles.

Now seriously, what do you think?

I don't like to think. You told me to let men do it for me.

Jesus. Listen, let me tell you what is under this cityscape here...

Warren worked on large paintings of street corners filled with musicians and chess players, his own work, while they worked. Sometimes, not very often, he sold them.

I'm saving money, see. They, the administrators of this joint, were about to toss this very good canvas in the dumpster with a lot of others.

But why?

It already had a painting on it. I stopped them just in time.

You mean it was someone's canvas that used to paint here?

Yes. It wasn't a very good painting, but he sweated over it just like me. And I knew him. He died right here. Fell over at his easel.

It's how I'd like to go, says Henrietta. Fall right over at my easel. In fact, I'm planning it.

Oh, please, says Mike.

Well, if you do, there's someone'll come along paint over everything you've done. says Warren. And everything I've done except a miniscule one percent I sell. How's that grab you? I, personally, would never paint over a Henrietta Rose. I must say I admire her in spite of all, but who's to say, the fools that come along when I am gone. This guy I'm painting over here, I didn't happen to admire, but I knew him, I remember him. And who's to say that some fool comes along after I'm gone and wants a cheap canvas.

Well, at least they won't go in the dumpster, like the trash we make of colored paper at the Sunshine Club. At least it's decent canvas, she. And maybe one day someone will be looking for a Warren, clean it off, and find it underneath.

Ha ha! that's a good one!

Ha, ha, yourself; it's happened.

What a conversation, Mike says. He has neighbors that buy all his paintings. People like to see all the hairs painted on squirrels, and falcons with every feather. And also he has fifteen grandchildren and they hang his paintings in their bedrooms...Mike knows what his public wants.

She thinks maybe she should take some of her better things to West Boylston. She'll hang them there among the cranberry sifters, antique breadboxes, printing presses, yes! Contribute to all the *stuff* in the world! Why shouldn't she? Mounty's counting on some of it having value. Yes. She sees his project, at that moment, in a new light.

How much stuff that hangs now, in museums, passed through hands like Mounty's, lay for years in places like the house in West Boylston? Too big to sell, a realtor told her once when—out of idle curiosity, she had no real intention of selling—she looked into selling the house.

Must go out there, question Mounty. Of course, if the house ever falls in Charles's hands. She'll have to see it won't. She'll have to talk to Mounty.

Between them they have two heirs that she knows of. Owen, and Mounty's daughter Isabel. Isabel is fruit of a marriage that lasted seven months when Mounty was nineteen.

She must find a way to deal with Jason, Henrietta Rose thinks as she walks beneath the Waltham Savings revolving sign which flashes its bit of Reality Orientation:

THE TIME IS 3:14…
THE TEMPERATURE IS 39
DEGREES FARENHEIT…

She feels in her pocket for bus fare and finds the label from the cat food box. The cat is going hungry from her forgetfulness. She goes in the supermarket to pick up the lamb and rice variety that Geoffrey favors, then some nice pink grapefruits on sale. She turns a corner to take a peek at relishes, picks up Greek olives, and The Kisser in his Red Sox uniform steps sideways from behind a table of special sales of damaged can goods, smacks her on the lips. Ah well. He doesn't look as fresh and clean as usual, must have his problems of daily life the same as other wanderers in the streets. He doesn't carry his possessions in a supermarket cart like some, so he must have a room somewhere to keep his baseball suits and other uniforms, she speculates.

They both continue on their way, he with a look of satisfaction. I'm too easy, Henrietta thinks. I always was.

She never had a lot of boyfriends before Gerald. Lutie worried, waited, a bit impatient, it seemed to Henrietta. Sweet Briar College, which she entered without question—it was where the Montague women went to get a suitable husband—seemed to fail her, though she went on all the weekends, ended close to being compromised a couple times.

Like the time a boy named Clayton Braddock the Third invited her to a frat party and they arrived at an empty house:

But where's the party? She.

The party's you and me, said Clayton Braddock the Third.

She didn't feel stupid till he brought her home; she'd been too busy delaying him with conversation. He wants a party, she thought, I'll give him one; and she told him stories of Lutie and the Bears and of her experiments with Mounty. It worked. He wasn't as sure of himself in the role of seducer as he'd thought he'd be; and there was always a lingering whiff of the southern gentleman in those boys. She thinks it was that evening she discovered her powers of conversation. Scared her though, the close call; and afterward she transferred to the State University back up north, and met Gerald, who needed none of the arts of those southern boys to induce her to slip off her panties under the bushes outside Howland Hall, where his father who was the chairman of the chemistry department, held forth to freshmen.

Gerald was their only child, born to a woman who died the year he was thirteen. It was a very competent family; they hardly ever had a meal together, yet possessed a certain solidarity in their dedication to the sciences. She'd meanwhile—being bad at mathematics—given up her love of stinking messes, and majored in English literature.

Her alchemist. Her English literature mind was more agile than his in certain ways and this intrigued him. She laughed at him a lot, and he had never been laughed at before. He considered her friends dangerous bohemians. They were reading Aldous Huxley's *Doorways to Perception*, seated on the floor of her friend Jack's littered attic room. Jack, alone of them, had escaped the dorms. They drank a lot of beer up there, the empty cans rolling among the candles stuck in wine carafes, picking up and browsing in the drifting pages of a novel Jack was writing. Gerald found the mess appalling, while she found it exhilarating.

Aldous Huxley, she can see it now, was opening the doors to the coming culture of hallucinogens, which would be in its full flower when her sons and daughters were in their early teens. The beer drinking, on the other hand, harmed her not at all; nor did the drugs, like mescaline, that they talked about and longed to try. They never got their hands on any.

Funny, how she'd ignored this Doorway. But she wasn't suffering, then, the despair that gripped her after, after she was twenty-five and living in that apartment in Philadelphia, with no furniture, not sleeping well. It was later she entered that other doorway suggested by Gerald's pharmacology textbooks. She wasn't drinking at all, then. Gerald wasn't a drinker; it wasted time. He needed his wits about him at all times. And of course she wasn't patronizing pharmacies as yet; that took the move to other continents and another couple years to acclimate herself, and plumb the depths of sleeplessness she was capable of.

But why was I so easy by the time that Gerald? Had Clayton Braddock broken me almost down, though we didn't know it? Or was it that she knew Gerald would marry her, while Clayton Braddock the Third probably would not?

She's back, with her parcel under the Waltham Savings.

ANCIENT ORDER OF HIBERNEANS
ANNUAL CORNED BEEF DINNER
BENEFIT SCHOLARSHIP FUND...

At the Sunshine Club Becca gives them one of those personality quizzes.

So we'll know what we want to be when we grow up, Henrietta titters.

Now, Henrietta, Becca scolds, putting a good face on it. She could put a good face on a mackerel.

What is your favorite body of water?

Bobby chooses Lake. Henrietta says River. All the others choose Ocean.

She says river because she likes to think of all the towns The Charles runs through until it reaches the great harbor, but another day she might choose Ocean. This is so silly.

Becca pursues. What do you think of when you open your refrigerator? Eating, Cleaning, or cooking?

Cooking of course. Bobby says Eating.

So silly. Of course Bobby doesn't have to worry about growing up.

She remembers the personality test Carol told her about: Is the Bible a work of Literature or of Divine Revelation?

You could ponder that for a lifetime. Not a fair question.

She would have refused to answer it. Messing up their dumb test. This would have been back when she was supposed to be growing up. Unlike Bobby, Henrietta Rose had no excuse for not growing up.

This thought humbles her, and she tries to humor Becca and answer the questions seriously.

Would you rather go to the beach or the mountains for a rest.

Will there be people at the beach? Berta asks.

Just say the first answer comes in your head, Becca says.

They all say Beach, but Henrietta changes hers to Mountain.

That night she wakes out of a dream before dawn and realizes she's been to a place she's been before. In reality? She searches her memory.

No, it's a crazy place that couldn't exist in reality, but it's a place she goes often, she recalls, and following Carol's suggestion from the Jung Institute, she fixes it visually.

She's going to the city.

You can go two ways: through a vast ruin of windowless buildings, some roofless, others almost intact and occupied. Terrifying dead ends of miserable little manufacturing shops and sellers of soft drinks and rotten vegetables and roots for cooking. Or derelict manufacturing plants. No way through them. She had just wakened in one of them.

But she can recall other routes that involve a tiresome ferry boat to cross a body of water. You must enter a maze of dark corridors to purchase a ticket at a tiny blackened window and wait. Once across you are routed to an underground chamber of fast moving trains and purchase another ticket at another discreet window. Then cross lines of tracks to find your train; she never finds hers.

Is this where she is, at a dead end?

But she's so happy with her life.

It's necessary to figure out your dreams. No matter how ridiculous they are, Carol used to say.

What a bother.

Then Mounty calls. Kate has stopped in at the old house, looking for her.

Kate!

She had a child with her, but no husband. He gave her some money and her mother's address.

A child?

A girl, about five. Very shy.

Henrietta has to sit down.

She seemed happy to get some money. Said she'd only call her mother if something didn't work out...

A child.

If what didn't work out?

She didn't say. Mounty, like their father was incurious about other peoples' doings.

Her heart is fluttering. She fixes herself some tea, using tap water in her hurry. Then stops herself and goes for the filter pitcher, moving slowly and taking time to butter a corn muffin she's brought home from the market. I must take care of myself.

A child.

Kate.

Kate was the most normal of her children, competent, but not outstanding in any direction. And persevering and strong. Like Carol, she had the Rose good looks. She took herself off with one of the weak boys she seemed to attract, got a good job, rose to a high position, studied at night, and that was the last Henrietta knew.

Next day Becca gives them the results of the quiz. Bobby would be happy as a postman. Berta, a kindergarten teacher. And one of the things Henrietta should be is a cruise director. Of course this will never happen, Becca explains, a bit dismayed, Henrietta thinks, by finding herself so removed from Reality. But it was fun, wasn't it? she asks them. Albert, at that moment, is sliding his hand into his pants and requiring Becca to retract it an hold it in her lap.

A cruise director.

Or an actress. Well, that makes a little sense. All her life she's been on a stage.

She has the dream again, wakes to ponder it at exactly five am. It was different this time. It seems there is another route, rural and rather pleasant, involving a climb up a soft green hill, and a walk over a bridge with no ticket required. She was being led by someone. Her daughter Kate, she thinks at first, but by the end it has become someone else... Who?

Later, having gotten up to the bathroom, and having a drink of water, she recalls; it is the odious cousin Nancy she used to be required to play with alone, without Mounty around to get them in trouble.

No use trying to go back to sleep, she lies in a drowse, the dream teasing her.

The hard parts first, she thinks about her harp lessons. Were the first two dreams about that.

And this new pleasant dream about the rest of her life...?

How nice.

And she is to be a cruise director! Ha ha.

"Don't be confused by surfaces. In the depths, everything becomes law, and those who live the mystery falsely and badly (and they are very many) lose it only for themselves and nevertheless pass it on like a sealed letter without knowing it."

Carol had written this quote from Rilke in the notebook Henrietta found in her suitcase after she died. She has since copied it into her own notebook, on the back pages and sometimes reads it.

Unlike Bobby, and Berta, and Albert, Henrietta has no excuse not to grow up.

A cruise director
Those who live the mystery falsely and badly...
My daughter Kate may call any day.
These thoughts drive her out of bed.

I'll have a dinner party! She suddenly decides, once she's dressed and has her cup of tea and slippers on her chilled feet. The elation accompanying this is familiar. Dinner parties were how she used to put right scandals, spats, resulting from her having too much *Ron de Caldas* at her last dinner party. Well, it won't be like that this time; but Henrietta Rose can throw a dinner party with her hands tied behind her back, with her heels up to her fanny, with her brain blinked out.

It happens Jason, who used to live in Boston, has moved the next town over, to Newton. She's called him several times and been invited to a couple stiff occasions with his family. This occasion must be on her own ground, and must be but the first of a series. She writes the invitation then and there. Then plans her menu:

Baked potatoes in their jackets. Fresh vegetables, an aspic salad, little fillets mignon, broiled to turn, and bloody.

Jason calls midweek. He guesses they can come; but does she really feel...? She really feels. On other occasions she's tried to question him about Owen's condition. This time she doesn't mention it.

She doesn't buy her meat and vegetables until the day before the dinner. The preparation sequence is all spelled out in her notebook: Make the aspic early morning. Put potatoes in at four and turn out the aspic. Boil stringbeans at five and butter them. Saute the mushrooms at six, no earlier; and don't do steaks until guests arrive.

She sets the table in the kitchen corner she's made pretty with a bookshelf and a rocking chair. She only has two kitchen chairs for the table, has to drag in dressing stool from bedroom for the third.

A little dinner, nothing more, an opening, she tells herself when nerves threaten. The corner pleases her. She makes a centerpiece of gourds, apples, pears, some walnuts. They'll talk of superficial...well when did Henrietta Rose have trouble making conversation? A little wine for Jason? No. She'll make a point of that, and show herself to them giddy on grape juice. The *Ron de Caldas, Bwana Bap*, was never necessary; she can see it now.

A dinner party, nothing more, but first of many, she'll suggest. She needs the practice. They must help her by being her first guests.

At two thirty, Jason calls and asks if he can bring a woman along. She's struck dumb, then calculates quickly she has extra steaks and aspic, but stammers that she has only three chairs. He says he has some folding chairs, that she can have them.

She sets another place. Her son-in-law hasn't any notion of tact; he never did. He is a scientist, like Gerald. Gerald used to appreciate him, the few years that he knew him. Well, she thinks, he has a woman and was embarrassed at first to tell me. It's all right; I have risen to worse occasions. After she puts in the potatoes and pretties up the butter dish, she spends some time working at her frizzy hair, her face, her dress, her earrings, mostly so she won't be tempted to put the stringbeans on and rush the mushrooms. She doesn't want anything to acquire that overcooked and tasteless quality of the dinners at the Sunshine Club. She checks the aspic, rubs a clove of garlic over the steaks. It's lucky that she bought an extra. Jason must forgo a second steak. She's made a chocolate cake for Owen. She remembers he was a greedy little boy, much like Charles, but never fat.

They come at five-thirty. She gives them crackers and grapejuice, excuses herself to put the steaks on and put some butter on the beans and a small flame under.

Owen is looking handsome; and, as it happens, she finds the woman, whose name is Sheila, charming. She's too good for Jason, Henrietta thinks. Just like Carol. When did their relationship start? she wonders. Does this woman know the circumstances of Jason's leaving Carol? No, of course not; there probably was not a woman until later. Jason simply chose not to pass through Carol's dying by her side.

A "sealed letter," it was passed to her.

A bit of a strain, thinking of guests and timing the steaks all at once. She decides to put the steaks in Jason's hands, gives him the timer. He's pleased. He goes into the kitchen to turn the steaks and to set up the two chairs he's brought; and so she's able to chat with the woman, meantime, observe Owen. He seems a bit stunned—by medication, she assumes—but healthy, a good looking fifteen year old.

He enjoys his steak, which Jason manages to get just right the way Gerald used to, and plays with his aspic and string beans. He'd missed a year of school, was only this year starting high school. She remembers seeing him at the funeral; he was twelve, and looking pale, strung out, contending with voices. She'd still in her possession, back then, books that Gerald studied from at Temple thirty years ago; and of course, read everything they had to say about this schizophrenia. Dementia Praecox they called it. It wasn't till she noticed Gerald's books still had a chapter on the old Sister Kenney treatment for polio that she threw them out.

Patience, she tells herself. This is only the first of many dinners, and proceeding nicely. The woman, Sheila, praises the aspic. She could never do an aspic right, she says. The secret's parboiling the vegetables, Henrietta says, and reducing the tomato juice. I forgot it isn't probably, something boys go crazy over, she says to Owen, and he grunts. He was a tremendous talker, she remembers, when he was three or four. She wishes she could offer him the extra steak that's gone to Sheila, but there will be the chocolate cake.

And if it's thinking of his mother has him so subdued, well she respects it. Let his father comfort himself with new women; she would get her grandson back. She always knew that blood was thicker than marriage bonds.

But I'm not even related to you! Lutie used to cry when Franklin became coltish over her return from one of her rests.

I'm sure the Newton schools are very good, she says.

Oh, yes. We're very happy with them, Sheila says, implying she's moved in; of course it would be natural.

Sheila has an eight year old, says Jason.

Oh, I'm sorry. I might have asked him as well if I'd known, and I do appreciate the chairs.

We left her with a babysitter and she's quite content; she has the tele and all, says Sheila, a woman with social skills at least, if Jason lacks them. He's looking about her rooms now as if there's something she's forgotten to put on the table.

Of course, the wine, the cocktail, the social oil. I must apologize, she says. No wine. It seems I am an alcoholic. She rolls her eyes to indicate dire possibilities that might ensue if she had a bottle in front of her. She doesn't want to belabor this, and simply adds: It was in the family, my mother and my uncles you know, she says for Owen's benefit. Blood speaking to blood, she thinks, and has to stop herself from saying more.

Ah, is that so, says Jason, thoughtful, as if he's recalling events that this new knowledge might explain. But is this first time she mentioned it? Those calls she made last year, she tried to tell him, didn't she? But maybe he didn't take it in then since it didn't accompany his being deprived of his drink with dinner.

As happens with all her dinner parties, she's eaten without tasting, and is amazed how quickly it is over and it's time to serve dessert. She clears with Sheila's help, and slices the cake, large piece for Owen. It fills her with pleasure to see him put it away, ask for another. Must take care to fuel your growth, she teases him, recalling quantities of food it took to fill out Charles's six foot five.

Owen will be taller than either of his parents, she says; this Sheila must excuse the reference to Carol. In view of Owen's existence, we can't act as if she never was, now can we? she tells herself.

But she won't push it. She urges them into the sitting room and brings out her albums from India: Thought you'd like to see your grandma on an elephant, she says, and opens it before Owen.

Oh, you were in Africa, cries Sheila.

No, India. She opens album to a shot of Gerald standing by an English cottage from the time of Raj; it had been quite recently vacated and was being turned to some new use that had to do with Gerald's quasi-governmental post. A kind of residence inn, I believe.

More English than England, these old neighborhoods; and in our horror at things Indian, at times we'd take a picnic out by the old Lines, they called them, and we'd sit for a while in English gardens. But I got over this nostalgia sooner than Gerald, and later I made him take me places that had a kind of fearful beauty, like entrances to Hell, I used to think, those temples.

She turns some pages. Here, if you look closely, you see this monkey in the trees, and here's a piece of fallen temple, I must have taken this photo; Gerald always had to have a person in his, preferably a relative... Here's one of his, with me in front of some Nawab's palace, turned into a lovely, really, guesthouse, where we stayed once. And here's Gerald's plant with him in front...He made a kind of very nutritious flour supplement supposed to be for the poor to add to their chapatis...

Henrietta relaxes for the first time. The stress of dinner over, she's delighted at finding such a safe, appropriate subject for the remainder of the evening, which hasn't been so simple as she expected, but which she feels she's handled magnificently.

What's this? Owen asks, picking out a photo that's not fastened in.

Oh, that's San Mateo. That belongs in the other album. I got careless, I suppose...

But what is it?

Oh, it was thrilling. That's in Venezuela. We were there before we went to India, she explains for Sheila. San Mateo was the hacienda of Simón Bolívar. He went there with his tutor after his mother died. And then returned, after he was grown up and made up his mind to free the colonies, begun the struggle. He freed the slaves. No one in the world had freed a slave before.

Oh, it was a thrill to come upon it. They had left it abandoned over a hundred years, were just beginning to restore it. There were workmen who said we couldn't go in; they were repairing the roof beams. But we bribed them with a bottle of rum. So, they let us in. There were little cannons and cannon balls lying in the grass and there was grapeshot imbedded in the doors. I dug one out and have it still. She gets up and goes to the shelf and finds the old copper chocolate pot in which she's stored the little lead ball and also one of the hand-made nails that she'd pulled out of a roof beam.

Wow, says Owen, weighing the little ball in his hand.

There'd been a terrible battle there. The Spaniards were advancing and the colonists had stored their gunpowder in a warehouse next to the manor that had been used before the war to store the cane...I think it was cane; it was a sugar plantation. Oh, so beautiful, in the valley between the mountain ranges west of Caracas.

How do you know so much about it? Owen asks.

I loved Simón Bolívar, she says. You felt him everywhere. He crossed those mountains over and over; and one of the times he led a barefoot ragged army through one of the highest passes, in the snow, so that he could surprise the Spaniards.

Well, anyway, we walked through the manor. It was very plain as you see. Two towers—this one tumbling down—and empty except for a huge trunk at the base of one of the towers. That trunk, the workmen told us, had been filled with gold collected from colonists to pay for war.

And I read later how he'd come, the boy Bolívar, with his tutor, who was influenced in his theories of education by Rousseau. Rousseau believed that children ought to touch and taste and smell the world and learn from nature not from books, be free... They lived at San Mateo—just the two of them—very simply, the years after his mother died. And they went around and classified the plants that had no names yet even, this was such a new world..

Hmm, he says. Have you read Carlos Castañeda, Grandma? That's how he thinks—about the being free.

No, I haven't. She's glad to have this hint that he's a reader like his mother, but Jason shifts uneasily in his chair, one of the folding ones he's brought, refusing to sink into her couch like Sheila.

You must tell me sometime, about things you read, she says. But let me tell you the final...When we went outside again, we walked around some walls that were falling into a lovely rubble of shards of clay and stones and a mixture of dung and mud and straw they built with in those days—I still remember the lovely color of it—and the and little channels that brought water to the kitchen I suppose; and then we walked around the ruins of the storehouse, came upon a little marble plaque, flat to the ground, that told about the soldier, named Ricaurte, who'd caused the explosion of the powder. He'd shot his pistol into it so it couldn't fall into hands of the advancing enemy. Blown himself to bits. This was his grave.

And it looked, the whole place, as if nothing had happened in all the one hundred and thirty years since that war. As if that pistol shot had just rung out, and the explosion happened, and this was the silence that followed.

I'm sure it's changed now, she goes on, all restored and turned into a museum.

A triumph, Henrietta. Your dinner party... She whispers it, then she says it out loud to Geoffrey, who has come looking for his dinner now that they're alone again. A triumph! Oh if only Carol could have known...!

She straightens up the kitchen, leaves the quite presentable three folding chairs around the table, moves her more substantial ones into the sitting room; then surveys the scene of it shamelessly while planning future triumphs.

She had never shone, not quite like this, oh, well, she'd had her moments of charming this or that sales manager, vice president...what did it matter? Those evenings were merely a sharpening of her wits in preparation for this evening.

She'll never sleep tonight, she'll still be going over every minute of it when the dawn...she's sure of it; well never mind. There was the tiny awkwardness at the end, but nothing fatal: She'd gone with Jason into the hall to fetch the coats, and taken the opportunity to tell him she liked Sheila very much and to inquire if maybe Owen's medication was too much, perhaps; and Jason had said the name of it—perplexan, something like that—when Owen had come up behind them and, hearing the name of the medication, had cried: I hate it! It's a Fascist drug!

You have to have it if you're going to live with us, Jason had said grimly.

She won't think about that part. She oughtn't to have brought it up, and she'll know better next time.

It's four o'clock when she can finally stop herself reviewing the whole evening, and turn into what remains of the dark and sleep an hour.

Henrietta Rose takes the bus downtown, and walks to The Sunshine Club, next day, in spite of her sleepless night.

> THE JUBILEES A GOSPEL CHOIR
> TO SING AT THE FIRST BAPTIST
> CHURCH ON SATURDAY...

Announces the electric sign that goes around The Waltham Bank for Savings. She sees her neighbor, Chang, go weaving down the middle of Main Street on a bicycle; she must tell him Waltham is not Beijing, that he should stay on the side and wear a helmet.

At The Sunshine Club, she finds some pretty Brahms, arranged for harp, and plays a while before lunch. It pleases Megan, but puts the others to sleep and causes Albert to fall off his chair.

Disgusting, Megan says. I don't consider them even human.

Oh well, says Henrietta. Some of them were once; unfortunate, I'd call it. She wonders if another stroke could render Megan like her sisters, would she make the connection? No, of course, she wouldn't be able...How strange. One of God's jokes, as Carol would have it.

You know those messages they're sending from Arecibo, Megan tells her at the lunch table. It's another of Henrietta's social triumphs getting Megan to talk at table.

From Arecibo. I can't quite think...

The radio telescope.

Oh, yes.

Well they should get a response before the year twenty twenty-one, they say. If there is life out there, I'm hoping it will be before.

Ah, crikey, Mike explodes. These females and their infernal conversation!

I beg your pardon. Henrietta stares at him.

Pudding pie, says Adie, gabbling the pureed Swiss steak.

Maybe even in my lifetime, Megan perseveres. Though not much chance of it, although Carl Sagan, you know, believes it could be any day.

Goodness.

And the question of the missing matter in the universe...

Oh, dear. Is it important? Henrietta queries.

Important? It's a matter of whether all of it just flies apart, expanding infinitely, or whether it's contracting. It's such an urgent question, and no one even thinks about it, I mean except astronomers.

Well I shall certainly think about it from now on, says Henrietta.

The weather is warmer, a regular thaw, so she walks up Lexington toward the County Detox, where there's a meeting at five. John the Indian stops in his brown Plymouth Horizon and picks her up and drops her. He doesn't go in himself, because, in his opinion, this meeting is full of priests and murderers.

She's never met a murderer there, a couple priests, but they are everywhere, along with postal workers, used car salesmen, long distance truckers, and ex-nuns, to name a few. A lot of people from the Driving Under program come here, a few la de das from Lexington.

A little girl from Driving Under speaks first: gap-toothed, looks about sixteen, until you really study her. She only has a month or two, complains how hard it is to go to weddings in her Irish family, and funerals. But she is doing O.K. She lost a bunch of stuff, she says, but the Higher Power is taking care of her. She bought a little snake she saw in the window of a pet shop, thought that it might die; but now it's turned bright green and holds its head up, sticks its little tongue out. Jesus! I can take care of something, wow, you know, And myself too!

Yes! thinks Henrietta. The triumph of her dinner party is like some magical medium she moves in, makes her love this girl, love all of them, from this girl, from any murderers might be present, right back to the founders of this crazy jerrybuilt organization.

They talked about Bee Weeson at the meeting in Mexicali. They were so grateful for Bee Weeson, if it hadn't been for Bee Weeson...spoke a young laborer with his name embroidered on his workshirt one night when she had gone after Carol was asleep. She didn't know, at first, who they were talking about, then suddenly it dawned:

His picture, and that of Doctor Bob were hanging on the wall in front of her—high up, where, at the clinic, they hung the holy pictures. Yes of course, Bill Wilson, he is also theirs, she'd thought.

They brought her cups of super-sweetened coffee, never allowing her to get up and serve herself. Finally, she told them she didn't like sugar in it; and, though doubtful that anyone could drink coffee without sugar, they brought it to her the way she wanted, warning any newcomers not to put sugar in the *companerita's* coffee. That's what they called her, the little comrade.

The meeting wasn't too very different from those across the border, except for the speaker's table being like a little altar, and the fact that they bantered with the speaker. They weren't undisciplined however, just more centrally organized; and, when the bantering got out of hand, the chairman, Victor, who also wore a dark blue shirt with his name embroidered on and that of his company, tinkled a little silver bell that stood at the speaker's table, and brought them to order. They were so tender toward her and so happy, and had such appalling stories, for some of them were not Mexicans, but Guatemalans, and they had experienced terrible things, like seeing their fathers beheaded and hanged from trees in the conflict there.

There was a vocabulary to be learned before she could make sense of what she heard. *Lagunas mentales* (mental lakes?) were blackouts. She had a wild poetic notion of a black pool with the moon reflected at the bottom. Much later she found out that the word was "lacunae." *Goma* was a hangover, or at least one of the terms. Themselves, they called The Brothers or The Comrades. She was The Little Sister, or The Little Comrade.

She told them about Carol in a broken way. They had their wives or sweethearts lighting candles for her in the churches. When the language came back to her a bit, she stood up on her legs at the little altar, spoke of her drinking. It must have sounded preposterous to them, for a woman never admitted to drinking in that culture, and none ever came to these meetings. It was so novel, to be the only one. She found herself even flirting mildly with them; couldn't help herself, she found them so attractive, even though the oldest, must have been Carol's age at most.

No women, no old men. But in my country, half of us are women. Yes, they told her; women drank there; but society wouldn't allow them to admit it.

Victor was the most attractive, the one who rang the little bell, looked stern, and lectured them about the cleaning up, about Service, who remembered always to bring her coffee and to warn the others about no sugar in it. And he had such a sly smile. He reminded her of someone, she recalls. Who is it?

XIV

The thought of Victor, the sly smile, occupies her on and off through a week of bitter cold and snow during which she stays home and suffers an entire day of her landlords, Mr. and Mrs. Fahey, walking in and out of her apartment looking for the frozen pipe that's caused a leak in their livingroom downstairs. She shuts herself away in her kitchen and drinks endless cups of tea while Mr. Fahey removes a section of her bathroom tile. The present irritation becomes too much for Henrietta Rose and while drinking her twentieth cup of tea and trying to avoid the attentions of Mrs. Fahey who continues to tell her about her grandson with the "photogenic" memory and her daughters who seem to be able to purchase anything under the sun, it suddenly comes to her who Victor's sly smile reminded her of. It is Jacinta.

The third year of their marriage Gerald was posted to Antioquia, which was coincidentally one of the places he'd grown up in, during his own father's many academic postings. From the age of twelve through seventeen he'd attended the Britanica in Lomas Altas where his father taught chemistry; there, he'd acquired a good education, Spanish fluency, and a Venezuelan stepmother—she'd been assistant headmistress and had wooed his lonely father.

Henrietta knew only two things about these years: that they had been a time when Gerald went "a bit native," and had the only escapades of his life. You don't know what it's like when your father's always your headmaster, he told her. During his senior year, he'd actually caused a servant girl to conceive a son, and was still sending small amounts of money to the girl. As the years went on it became more and more difficult to believe this of Gerald.

When they moved to Tula, he went ahead of her. She had to go home to nurse Lutie for a month after one of Lutie's "rests," and then she flew alone, down to that foreign place. A giddy thing, she obtained a bargain flight out of Miami, Lloyd Aereo Colombiano. Roundtrip required by her hasty visa. She remembers she filed away the return, in case in case… Marriage, like everything else, seemed precarious those days. She also bought a hat, her first, the kind Rose Kennedy used to wear.

The DC4, sat on the runway like a little begging dog between the Constellations. You had to climb the aisles; and, though the little plane took almost vertically to the air, it rumbled very low, and very slow above the blue-green Caribbean. She could see right to the very bottom; it made her high; her life unrolled before her hopefully. It happened to her on other occasions—once in India, once in the White Mountains—at a certain altitude. Sometime later, at a drunken party, she regaled a man about that flight, how safe she felt, flying so very slow and so very low…

You actually are safer flying very high and very fast, he said.

Then mountains, densely covered grayish green, solemn and foreign, range on range. That's one of ours down there, the stewardess pointed to a red gash, a fuselage against a mountainside. They were given fricassee of chicken on a paper plate and landed in Baranquilla where a humid breeze was wafted through the cabin.

He was waiting for her, the man she married, in the capital.

Take off that crazy hat you're wearing? he demanded. They hadn't seen each other in three months: she finished up a temp position in Philadelphia while he quit his job and vamoosed back to his mother's native land, avoiding a draft board set to send him to a war that wasn't his—it wasn't anybody's turns out later.

We are almost strangers, she thought as they checked into a hotel. She had checked into hotels wearing a fake wedding ring with Gerald, knowing him better than this husband who with absolute legality wrote Sr & Sra Gerald Rose in the great leather-covered register set before him.

It was all right once they were in bed.

Somehow they were back to the days he really was a stranger, dark to her light, unknown to her known. She opened to him fervently, and it seemed they must have saved up, in those months apart, the vital juices necessary to make the child they couldn't make back in Philadelphia. Of course she wasn't aware of this for two months.

A dictator had been overthrown. An enlightened novelist was president. Women had marched in the streets—Gerald's stepmother among them—to bring this about. To keep the wealth from pouring out of the country, imports were closed off. Products such as Band Aids, silver polish, astringent creams, had disappeared from shelves. Gerald, in his spare time, and an unemployed chemist from Ecuador, Amable Rosero, proposed to manufacture these products in an unused coffee warehouse in Bagua. They had started with Band Aids.

She went once to see this project, a rackety affair that reminded her of the Harold Lloyd films they used to see at the art museum. Amable, who was excruciatingly polite to her, struck her as a man accustomed to failure. His teeth were bad and his shoes had cardboard soles. At the end of an elaborate belt that looped up and down and around the cement block building, however, a passable Band Aid emerged, and Gerald was full of hope and plans.

In the meantime she must stay with his parents in a long narrow apartment over a hardware store in the city of Tula. They had once been rich and able to send their son to study in the U.S., but with the fall in coffee prices and Gerald's father's illness they were considerably less prosperous. There, in Tula, he became ill, after a career of teaching in three universities; and there they stayed.

The illness was a mysterious one. All of a sudden he became unable to work, filled with indecision and anxiety, able only to sit on the balcony overlooking the Cine Estrella across the street and rock back and forth in his armchair. The only things that could calm him were to be taken for rides in the car, and old gray Chevrolet, that Gerald's mother had bought and used for this purpose only; and to play one of the old card games he knew from before his illness. It was called *tute* and reminded her of some simple game of her childhood, like Go Fish. Gerald's mother, the fourth ranked bridge player in the country found these games excruciating; so Henrietta, a very indifferent card player, was employed to calm him with this strange deck of cards which had on them goblets, swords, thorny clubs and gold coins. Without aspiring to any more complex game, she found it as excruciatingly boring as Gerald's mother did. Meanwhile, the old man grunted with pleasure as he drew toward him the piles of dry red beans that represented tokens of his winnings, and dealt out another hand before the anxiety could set him rocking back and forth again..

It was awful, and Henrietta found her own uneasiness in this world returning to match his. The excitement of coming here had only briefly lifted it.

After breakfast the old man was taken every day for the same drive past the market and the provincial cathedral, out to the *ingenio* where he was shown the new machinery. The midmorning coffee was served every morning at eleven and then there was lunch and a nap. At three in the afternoon, there was another sitting down to *cafe con leche* and the skin of the boiled milk was ceremoniously picked off, *la nata*; and sometimes a boiled egg was eaten and sometimes an *arepa* with white cheese, and the cards were brought out. The sun went down behind the *cordillera* every day at six precisely, every day of the year, because they were so near the equator. When it was the rainy season, the rains came every day at noon.

But the worst was being only able to talk in short phrases. She could say: *The mountains are beautiful. It is raining again. The coffee is tasty. I have much pleasure in meeting you.* Always addressing everyone with *Usted*. The informality of the Coast did not reign here in those chilly mountains.

But she needed verbs. Gerald's mother saw her suffering, she thought, but it would have taken verbs to explore it. Once, long ago, Misia Mercedes taught English in a girls' academy. But it is *esfumado*, her English, she said..

She laughed and waved her hands. Henrietta caught her meaning. This was a woman she could like, she decided. For months she had hated everything: *tute, arepas,* boiled milk with the *nata* to be pulled off, red beans, rain, the mountains, the endless *boleros* played on radios in the street below. It was a miserable country, she had concluded, amazed at her disappointment. But they both made an effort.

I like that word, "*esfumado*", she ventured.

We have poet. He say most beautiful word in Spanish is *agotado.*

She was given the poet. She learned verbs. Still, it was not enough. She was in a Biblical despair. Like Sarah, like Rachel. Why was there no child? Like Carol, Henrietta's children were tardy in coming. The women who came to visit Misia Mercedes asked her right out. *Y los hijos?* They stood so close and said such intimate things to her. An invisible barrier that caused people to stand back in her own country wasn't perceived here. A cousin of Gerald's, who had been married five months and was already parading her belly, was pointed out to her. And you married more than a year....

I shall have to go, she told herself hysterically. She was becoming hysterical. A morning after Gerald left for the Band Aid factory, she took out the other half of her ticket from her suitcase and took it down to a travel agency she'd noticed on their drives with her father-in-law. But they were out of business, Lloyd Aereo. Shut down by the authorities. She recalled the fuselage lying against the mountainside.

She read the poet. She studied the verbs.

Her periods didn't come. She assumed it was the stress and the change of climate. Her mother-in-law observed her closely. I think you are *en estado,* she said. She looked up the expression. It could mean either in an emotional state or pregnant. She was just wishing for a grandchild, Hennrieta thought. Misia Mercedes was the only one of them all who seemed to stand back, to hesitate to come as close to her as even perfect strangers. She was grateful.

Her mother-in-law had her amusements: her bridge games, which were like solemn rites—Henrietta exposed her own slapdash bridge only once—her Piel Roja Cigarettes which she smoked in bed with the newspapers and the crossword puzzle spread out, her *comadres*: Alicia Bustamantes and her sister Louisa Meza, who came every day to cut out patterns for dresses based on the fashion pages of *Vogue.* Louisa had one dress brought from Paris, which was kept like a holy effigy in the huge black lacquer armoire in the hallway; and this dress, together with a convincing fake they had confected, was going to be the prime attraction for a dress shop they planned to open in Calle Bugalagrande. There were other bursts of enthusiasm, a period when she fired their cook, Nelida, and marched out to the kitchen to cook herself. Then a series of disasters, which led to Dalila who was a treasure.

Sometimes the bridge players relaxed with a game in which the red beans were not exchanged for money, and this was the one occasion she joined them. It was hardly a friendly game; but she was holding her own as Misia Mercede's partner, when Eulalia Llosa, who was playing opposite Bertha Meza said to her partner acidly as the cards were picked up for the next deal:

You should have kept your heart, Misia Berta. The spade would have been good. Berta said nothing, but her wattles shook as she paid the kitty. A sorbete of curuba had been slipped in among the cards and red beans and the ladies were drinking it absently. Misia Eulalia's eyes were glittering. How clearly she remembers this: the long narrow apartment, the red tiles that were mopped with petroleum every day...

Henrietta concentrated fiercely. The Treasure kept bringing in plates of food. Then play stopped briefly and Eulalia said to Henrietta.

Have you been married long?

Just a year, she said.

You must be behaving yourselves very well. I was starting on my second by that time.

Henrietta ignored this.

Perhaps you use something, Eulalia suggested so indiscreetly that she blushed. Henrietta had heard women discuss birth control on other occasions and discovered it is a subject in which they were abysmally ignorant.

You use the aspirin water, I suppose, said Eulalia, keeping at it in spite of her red face. How clearly she remembers: The long narrow apartment, the red leatherette chairs, the boleros being played below in the billiard parlor across the street.

Aspirin water? She was appalled.

Personally, I find it doesn't work, said someone who added that she didn't let her husband near her unless she had her period. Last week I woke up and found my nightgown on the floor and him on top of me; I got right up and jumped up and down on the bed. That will get rid of it, sometimes, they say.

Eulalie was more enlightened. They tell me there's a pill for straightening out the periods; you can get if you go to a doctor and say you're irregular...

The Pill, yes, said Henrietta. The cards had been dealt again, and she must concentrate.

My cousin told me this, said Eulalie. And the name of a doctor. I could give it to you if you want, she said to Berta.

Oh, yes, yes. I'm desperate. You won't mention this conversation to anyone, will you?

Henrietta felt giddy.

I suppose that's what you use, Berta put to Henrietta.

No. Something else, we used for a time.

Ah...

She was incapable of describing a diaphragm in Spanish.

Something, something like a cork, she stammered.

In your country are wonderful things, said Berta. If one were to go to the botica and ask about this pill, I suppose one might be reported.

And if you take this pill, can you still go to church? I doubt it.

Dalila, you don't hear this conversation, her mother-in-law said to The Treasure, who was removing the plates.

A compote was served. There was no supper after these games and they would go straight to bed.

She read the books from the glass-fronted bookcase in the dining room. There was a book of stories of Ernesto Hemingway in translation she could make her way through. Also a set of James Fennimore Cooper, a copy of Black Beauty, and some essays of Lin Yutang in translation. These she ignored and chose a novel by Pio Baroja, which she found quite charming in the few parts she could understand.

The old man was reading Spengler's the *Decline of the West* over and over. Perhaps it was part of his almost cosmic pessimism. Just as he wouldn't learn any new card games, he wouldn't read any other book.

In the matter of verbs, she was improving. She knew verbs about cooking, verbs about dress shops, verbs about winning red beans in card games, about exchanging them for money.

And on some occasions, she understood the dinnertable conversation. There was a pottery jug filled with water on the table for all meals that Mercedes referred to as the *poso de Jacob*, about which there was a story about a distant relative who was a priest and visited once from France.. When offered the jug, he poured a bit out into his glass and tasted, probably expecting wine.

Ah, water, yes...Perhaps water may serve for washing... was his comment preserved in family lore.

Estás en estado. Misia Mercedes told her again. She doubted it. Henrietta's was a cosmic pessimism, like the old man's. She noted the familiar form of the verb though. Mercedes had begun the ceremony known as *tuteándonos*.

I would not use it yourself yet, Gerald said.

Oh, heavens no!

Another word for pregnancy, she learned from her studies, was *embarazo*, A word that could also mean embarrassment. Well, for her, not to be pregnant was the embarrassment.

Gerald took her on a weekend trip to Manizales, which was about a thousand meters higher than Tula. Starting with this extra thousand meters, they climbed the additional few hundred meters to the spire of the unfinished cathedral. This was enough to provoke in her another of her moments like the one in the DC4 over the Caribbean. She felt the stresses and counterstresses of the naked interior of the unfinished spire. Like rib bones forming, the arches pressed up against each other, and rose. It was a true gothic cathedral, not so much beautiful as awesome in its tensile strength. You would have noticed this less in a finished structure. They doubt they'll ever finish it, Gerald told her. That's best, she thought. She looked through the ribs at the marketplace below. I will stop being afraid, she told herself. The rough stones all around dissolved into a blur. I am so happy, she thought, and a moment later woke in a white room with an annoying light in her eyes.

Está en estado, she heard someone say, then she heard someone congratulate Gerald that his son would be born in his homeland, eligible to be *presidente de la república* one day.

Then they moved to Las Vigas and came to live in a pink stucco apartment building on the edge of the city, overlooking the turn off to the Road to The Sea, the route to the port of Buena. She spent a few idle months, Then, with the baby coming, she decided she must see the country, starting with following The Road to The Sea to its end.

The problem with the Road to the Sea was its destiny, the town of Buena and its dirty reputation: town of tin roofed shacks, unsavory eating places. And heat. She knew exactly what it would be like, at least she ought to have.

But they went. It was the year of the pacification of the countryside, the *Frente Nacional*, that they went—the country also undergoing one of those leaps that characterized her life.

Starting at dawn, they were above the weekend farms with their bright roofs of red and yellow *Eternit* by ten. The pavement ended and the road turned steeply up.

She remembers the red gash in the mountainside, and the deep ravine below, and on the opposite slope, a Polar Beer sign lettered in white stones, the sun, above the *cordillera* now, burning her right cheek and forearm.

I wish we could go straight on, she'd said to Gerald, who was nervous about the road and didn't answer. They were to stay a day with his aunt, who lived in

El Retiro, which was in the mountains.

They crossed a river, climbed again, the gash now on their left. She remembers a metal cross beside the road, a hub cap hanging from it. Car went over, Gerald told her. She looked into the chasm, asked him if they recovered the bodies. Not usually, he told her.

There were small valleys where the *carretera* opened out, small settlements, mud houses—sun-baked and crazed like ancient china, thatch roofs caught up on sapling racks trimmed at the bottom like the thick bang she saw on children in this sierra, crude signs painted on their sides, raw aniline blue:

Heximine...Purge the Gut of Ascaris And Other Parasites...

Red cliffs crowded. Another metal cross. On that one hung a bicycle wheel. Pines and blue-green eucalyptus replaced the banana trees as they wound higher.

Amparo will expect us, Gerald answered her earlier question.

But we could stop an hour, go straight on... she argued.

No, he told her, they will be shocked if you don't stay. He meant to go ahead and check for places where she could be put up decently, return to fetch her.

There was a lovely village of whitewashed houses with black thatch, a square, a church. The grass bleached colorless. Her nature went out to this austerity; she'd never quite been able to love the sprawl and riot of the valley where he'd settled her in their pink stucco wedding cake.

Se Ven De Que So Café

A sign spelled out in syllables read on a house that fronted the *carretera*. A woman in a black fedora filled their thermos, sold them wedges of a farmer's cheese. They stood outside to eat it in the thin, cold air, and a child asked for the canteen that hung from Gerald's shoulder. He refused, and the child grinned and asked for the knife, which Gerald gave him, recalling too late it had been her gift.

It's all right. I wanted him to have it, she said.

The road wound down. The only growth on those sterile and chilly slopes was a small spiky plant with woolly blue leaves; they were called "*Frailejones*," Gerald said; they wore little sweaters to keep warm.

In Purificación, storekeepers were throwing pails of water on the streets to keep the dust down. Stalls were closing in the market. Mangos and papayas rotted in the sun; and from a billiard hall came music of Luis Berrios: *Cuando Tu Te Hayas Ido...*

A wooden-bodied truck that carried firewood was off the road with a flat tire; and a woman waited with chicken on a leash.

LIBERDAD PARA LOS PRISIONEROS DE EL CACIQUE was splashed up in faded aniline on crumbling walls everywhere.

They neared the *páramo*, and stopped to look: bleached earth, some dusty paddle cactus; a lizard twitched, dislodging a pebble, held immobile, staring.

Then they descended to El Retiro. Gerald's uncle's house was on the central square; Amparo showed them to the room her second son—then off in military training—used to occupy. As soon as Gerald had gone downstairs, she asked The Question: *y, los hijos?*

None yet, Henrietta answered, aware, as always, it wasn't up to standard.

But we're expecting in July. she added. Her eagerness to answer this rude question amused her.

Amparo was sure she wanted to rest after such a trip. But she didn't; she ran downstairs to seek out Gerald and they went out for a walk. Gerald asked her if she'd told.

Well, I mean her very second question...

Then he explained that if they knew about the baby and learned she meant to accompany him to the coast with no prior check to see if there was a decent place to stay, and something happened to this baby, they would all say that it was because they weren't careful.

She was shocked.

They turned into the plaza. She studied the carved doors of the baroque cathedral. Gerald's stepmother's people were from there. Lozanos, Escobars, Ochoas. Across the street was an equestrian statue of Simón Bolívar with a plaque commemorating the *pesos de oro*, horses, men that el Retiro had sacrificed to the cause of liberty, in 1813.

The streets were narrow. They had to walk in file, squeezed between the traffic and the house fronts. She looked into the entryways at tile walls and fretwork doors. Acacias folded their leaves to tiny fists as they brushed by.

When this baby's born, she thought, I'll tell him of the risk I took, the looking...

She imagined Simón Bolivar riding over the *cordillera* in 1913. They said his buttocks were worn to calluses when he died.

She thought it a fine city, she told them at the dinner table. She didn't know when she'd seen so many sights.

Yes, commiserated Amparo. One does become so tired...

Not a bit, she said, she only wished that they were going straight on tomorrow...both of them, that was... But they'd protested: One doesn't court discomforts, said the old man.

Yes, one worries, *hija mia*, A woman in Buena. Here they were so comfortable. They had everything that one could wish: two movie theaters, a town club and a country club, and the military; one felt so much easier with the military near.

Gerald gave her extra money in the morning to go to the market and buy some cookies in a tin box.

Petites beurres, tan gentil! You shouldn't have.

Amparo pulled two wooden rockers into the shade of rubber trees that lined the patio. The *muchacha* brought coffee and there were more sweet confidences while they drank the coffee, picking off the *nata* from the surface of the oversweetened drink. Always oversweet…

You must be patient, in Carambolos, a woman can be subject to indignities, Amparo counseled, patting her neck and shoulders with a napkin. It was the hour of heat, and so they went inside to rest. Perhaps she'd like a book. She was led into a little parlor where a bookshelf held some engineering texts, the Merck Veterinary Manual, a copy of *Black Beauty*, and a Spanish translation of *For Whom the Bell Tolls*. She chose the Hemingway and took it to the little room and stretched on the bed. Out on the little balcony, Amparo rested upon a daybed, and, in his den next door, the old uncle snored. She read a page or two and slept, awakened by a clatter of bells at four. There was another sitting down to coffee. Don Lauriano consented to eat a boiled egg, and Amparo to a bit of white cheese with *arepa*. They inquired if she'd slept. Oh, yes, she cried, ashamed. But it was fortunate, said Amparo. One passed the horrid time of day, and when one waked the air had been exchanged. Don Lauriano explained. The heat at noon created a vacuum that caused an updraft later; cool mountain air came rushing down. It seemed to be true. The leathery palms on the patio were flapping about, and the tablecloth billowing.

They were sitting down to dinner when Gerald came. There was a woman he'd found, who rented rooms. They would do. The woman's name was Jacinta Saenz. Amparo was sure she wasn't respectable; but Gerald insisted. The house was clean and there was a bath.

It won't be all that comfortable, he warned her when they were walking after dinner. Not like here.

Thank God! she'd cried.

The Road to the Sea wound down from El Retiro. At intervals you could look below and glimpse the little train pull round a curve, its rooftop crowded with baskets, coffins, beasts in cages. Leaves that had been dusty, dripped with moisture. Tree trunks were black with damp. A wild cat crossed the road. She remembers two nearly naked men struggling in a ditch to extricate a mule.

And then it opened out a bit; there was a river with a grassy bank, some shacks were painted baby blue and pink, and pasted up with pictures cut from magazines; and, in the doorways, women richly lolling, sticking out an impudent tongue or hip on which an infant rode. She had to laugh. So many infants, so many bellies. She'd heard that they delivered themselves by hanging from a rope tied to the roofbeam. She thought of coral snakes, of *endamoeba histolica*.

They found Jacinta throwing clothing back into a tin trunk open on the floor. In the dark doorway a servant hovered with a sullen face. Ah, you find us in the middle of this. You must excuse. I mentioned to this wretch that I was missing a pair of stockings and she becomes hysterical and brings all her trunks in here and empties them in the middle of the room. I mean nothing. She thinks I accuse her of stealing. Now she must leave, she says. She has made all this mess and she must leave me in the middle of dinner! Jacinta, in this flustered state, invited them in and promised them a beefsteak and some plantain. Gerald had gone to park the car while Henrietta waited in the front garden in a chair the woman brought.

There was a plaza opposite, where boys were finishing a soccer game in the last light. Jacinta brought her a plate of cottony *badea* pulp, and it was like a compress laid on her dusty throat.

Jacinta Saenz was not a respectable woman, according to Gerald's aunt. Her life certainly was not orderly.

The cursed girl was packing up to leave her, she told Henrietta, but she would be giving them their supper soon. Henrietta told her not to upset herself; they were in no hurry. Did you fire her...? She was curious to know.

Oh, no, it's her idea to leave me in the middle of the dinner, said Jacinta. She's turned the house upside down and made the dinner wait, so she must leave; it's very logical!

At this point they had both laughed, and she fell in love with Jacinta.

The supper! screamed Jacinta then and ran into the house. The servant girl was leaving, she explained to Gerald, and told him she wished she could help.

No, let her get calmed down, he'd said. They'd walk around.

They crossed the little plaza, took a narrow street down to the estuary. There was another little plaza there, ill-kept but charming, with vine-covered trellises. The gray, unknown, Pacific lay beyond a point of land. They would take a launch next morning, around the point to Juancho where there was a beach.

Quite suddenly, it was dark, and they walked back. All that was visible of the soccer players now were their white pants. The ball rolled toward them; Gerald picked it up, drop kicked it back. *Cigarras* droned in a large ceiba tree, and dropped their tiny excrement, like rain.

The supper was served, a child, Jacinta's eldest, called them in. They sat on the verandah, and were given beefsteak, rice with beans. She found it tastier than anything she'd eaten in that country yet. Jacinta came and went with dishes, her youngest slung upon her hip, secured there with a wide blue shawl. I have no friends, she thought. No friend but Gerald.

I'll help later, she told Gerald.

Was it so important to her? Yes, it was, she told him.

The concrete sink was filled with dirty dishes; pots were set on the stove to boil loose deposits of burnt soup. The cursed girl had hidden all the dirty pans inside the oven.

No, no, you mustn't help! cried Jacinta. She was ashamed, she moaned distractedly, her mind still on the faithless girl. She'd find another girl. There were girls that passed by in the street; but they'd no papers and they were dirty. It was too bad. This girl had had her papers, and she was clean, Jacinta admitted. She wasn't a bad girl. She just got frightened.

More trouble than they're worth, sometimes, Jacinta said. Some days the very soup tasted of her poison. The infant, in an older child's arms, began to sob and hiccup; Jacinta took it, slung it on her hip.

At least just let me hold the baby, said Henrietta; and this Jacinta allowed, passing her the sodden bundle. Have you children? Jacinta asked her then, and she remembers she didn't mind the question from this woman, and told her about the baby coming. She didn't remember when she'd ever held a baby. Perhaps it was the first time.

She told Jacinta Gerald had told her they shouldn't stay here the next day, that it was too awkward, and they would find another place. The woman touched her cheek: Ah, mi nena...you stay, Jacinta told her, but must not work. She would die of shame!

All right, she agreed. She walked out to the patio with the infant, soothing it, allowing the mother to bring order to the kitchen. Above the patio wall, plantain leaves moved and gently touched in the soft wind. She found a square of flannel on the clothesline; lay it out on a pine table and, taking off the sodden diaper, wrapped the child in it, feeling pleased and solemn.

The child cried the moment she put him down; but stopped when he was in her arms again. Then the servant dragged her tin trunk to the kitchen, along with several cardboard boxes, not tied up: Here were her things. One could see that she stole nothing!

Ah the devil with you and your boxes! Leave my kitchen! screamed Jacinta, and the infant wailed. The girl was pale and dignified. Her brother was coming for her in his taxi, she said.

Bien, bien, I bear no grudge, Jacinta, bending over pots, said to her guest. She is good family; they're the worst.

Then came the conversation when she mistook her Spanish verb. They had spent some more time in the kitchen while the taxi-driving brother came to pick up the pale and dignified girl; and, after she'd gone, Jacinta talked about her humorously but kindly. She had been with her a long time. The girl's mother used to work for Jacinta, it seemed, when the girl was a child. They called her Luz then; and she was being taught to play guitar, so she could enter the Miss *Estado Arango* competition at fifteen and save them all with the prize money. When she was twelve, she worked there with her mother. Even then, she painted and used creams, flitting like a fairy, dusting, sweeping, afraid to break one of her long, polished nails. A spook, Jacinta's husband called her. Henrietta became curious about the husband.

Is your husband in the army? she asked.

They told you that? He's in the barracks, yes, Jacinta said evasively. How long have you been married, *nena*? she asked.

Well, we've been together seven years, Henrietta said. That is we are not married...

She had meant to say "we were not married"—meaning in the first three years they spent in Michigan for Gerald's graduate school—mistook her Spanish verb...as she often did those days. But Jacinta had interrupted with a confession of her own:

Ah, well, I'll tell you then, he neither is my husband, nor is in the barracks. He's the father of a number of these brats. My man, who left, just after that one you're holding, for the barracks, it is true. A month ago, however, they came looking for him, officers, they told me they can't find him. So, *mi nena*, we are sisters!

Yes, sisters, she'd said. It was still possible, of course, to change the verb, explain; but, since mistake had been the agent of this breaking of a barrier, of this desired intimacy, she was silent, thinking how, while she loved Gerald as much as she thought possible, she needed this, this woman for a friend.

Let me help you with the babies, she'd said. She was going to have a child, she needed to learn, she told the woman..

Ah, *nena*, Jacinta touched her cheek. You'll soon enough have problems of your own. Not that I won't be glad of you a couple days.

If Gerald understood, she thought, he would forgive...

The child had finally gone to sleep, and the pots were finally all washed, Gerald seemed to have gone to bed, so they sat in the parlor and Jacinta told her more about the girl who had left her, about her problems.

She had nothing in common with this person, Henrietta thought.

So tell me, *nena*, why he wouldn't marry you? Jacinta asked then; and, amazingly, a second lie came unhesitant to her lips:

Well, there's another woman, Henrietta said. He's already married.

Jacinta nodded..

And of course it was true that there was another woman. But it was the woman Gerald made pregnant when he was in high school—not Henrietta—that Gerald couldn't marry.

It's something never occurred to me, Jacinta murmured, that I should have a little *Norteamericana* for a friend.

But why should it be strange? Henrietta wanted to know.

Jacinta thought a moment: Fab Soap, she said. That's all I ever knew about your country: it's where they make Fab Soap! And atom bomb! And dollar! Henrietta was looking at her stupefied.

It's that we are so poor. We look at you and that's all that comes into our heads, that we are poor.

But, many people here are rich. Henrietta countered. Gerald's people are rich...

But they are few, and have the shame of all the rest of us. They can't forget about us, though they'd like to.

You and I, though... said Henrietta, I mean I will give up my claim to atom bombs if you'll give up...

Her shame? It wasn't so easy, she was thinking. But they would try! She would write to Jacinta, and they would see each other..."

Yes, perhaps. A child ran by; Jacinta grabbed him by his shirttails and hauled him off to bed. The power went off at ten, so she must take the candle, Jacinta advised.

Henrietta undressed in the dark and lay beside the sleeping Gerald. As she turned to snuff the flame, the child stirred inside her, the first time.

They walked the next morning, to the smaller of the wharves to take a public launch to Juancho. The green fringe of the land came right to the water's edge. In front of it, was a line of wooden shacks on stilts. They landed below a rickety pile of boards, and were told the launch would come back for them in five hours. The heat, which she had hardly noticed earlier, was now a palpable presence, like molten metal.

They crossed the coarse black sand to find a place to change, chose one of the many shacks. On the verandahs, fish was being fried. They had to order something to have a room to change in. A Japanese of middle age attended them; and Gerald ordered *aguardiente* for himself, cafe con leche for her. The *aguadiente*, brought immediately, was served outside. Her coffee was so long in coming that she walked inside to a large central room that served as kitchen, parlor, bedroom, where the Japanese resided amid remarkable confusion. She remembers one corner filled, inexplicably—for there was no electricity—with appliances, all new in boxes. Another corner was filled with oriental dolls.

He poured her coffee, set it on a tray, then cleared the cot of dolls and signaled her to sit. She told him she wanted to go outside with her husband, but he insisted: No, here. and, without asking if she wanted sugar, put three teaspoons in her cup. Oh, well, she would be amenable and drink it quickly. She complimented him on his pretty things, thinking of the oddity of the Spanish language being the only link between them.

Contrabando, he said. I buy in the Port. That explained the dolls, the Osterizer, and the fry pans. Imports had been closed on such things for a year. The word "*contrabando*", passed between the natives like a dirty penny, was tendered to her, another foreigner, conspiratorially.

She went to a back room to put her bathing suit on. Through the moist, loose-fitting boards she saw the jungle dark behind. Again, the second time, the child stirred.

And so at last, she walked across black sand to the Pacific Ocean. Tub-warm, leaden, barely breaking into waves. She walked in the water until it came up to her neck. Some dugout boats, slant-rigged like sampans, passed her slowly with their drowsy fishermen reclining in their hulls. She swam diagonally to the mouth of a small river, then walked back along the sand. Some fishermen were "walking" their long dugouts down the beach by swinging, alternately, one end forward, then the other. She found Gerald and their blanket. He'd bought the bottle of *aguardiente* from the Japanese, and also an outrageously expensive can of sausages.

Contrabando. They were too salty for her. She felt slightly ill, besides. She flopped down flat, her hip and shoulder touching Gerald's flesh, turned coppery already. The water felt like being in a womb. Everything was body temperature. A boy brought them a coconut with the top lopped off so that they could drink the milk by tipping it up over their mouths. The milk was cool, reminding her of the *badea* pulp Jacinta had served her the evening before. Was it only a day before? The conversation while Gerald slept seemed at that moment to have been hallucination.

Recalling Jacinta's narrow face, dark eyes, quick mouth, the small neat figure, slightly humped from carrying a child on her hip, she wonders what it was that she'd desired from the woman? She'd probably never write the promised letter, nor receive what would have been the barbarous reply spelled out in syllables:

Se ven De Que So Cafe.

But at that moment, she sat up and put a towel across her, worried about too much sun. Gerald, the betrayed Gerald, lay motionless, always more contented on a beach than she. And she'd thought how she would suffer, once the somnolence of that day was past. She would suffer for her fictions of the night before. Why had she always felt convinced that lying was a woman's vice? Her husband never lied, she knew. Merely kept silent sometimes, to satisfy certain social necessities...

But hadn't she kept silent, simply, having created a certain misunderstanding with a verb? But she'd been ready to embroider it. Embroidery was woman's work. And she had wanted it so much, been so convinced this woman, this Jacinta whom Victor in the AA meeting in Mexicalli reminded her of...

But at that moment she wanted nothing. Unless it was for Gerald to make love to her: lengthily, indolently, humidly, without her having to stir a muscle. Right then, right there, right on that beach, or in the water, it didn't matter. If Gerald were to turn over right then and take her, and then leave her, irresponsibly, with child...to deliver herself alone, hung on a rope thrown over the roofbeam...

If he were to paddle off in one of these dugout boats, and only return years later to give her another, she would wait in a dark shack for him to come, the child to come, her blouse unbuttoned, giving suck...

She was about to ask him if the little room she'd changed in might be theirs to use for other purposes, when suddenly she felt such an uprising of nausea she ran across the sand into the water, brought up the coffee, and the crackers, standing in the water to her waist, and watching bits of cracker float away...

Of course. Of course, of course, of course...

Jacinta was the woman Gerald couldn't marry.

Then the Little President was born. This was Charles. Her first born. When she went with Gerald to the Band Aid factory he lay in a little basket in the shade of a Ceiba tree.

Some things changed. A cousin who had been studying medicine in France visited and prescribed some new pill for the old man; and inside of a week, notwithstanding the literature that came in the bottle saying that it would take months, he was back to his old self, enjoying his rides, sitting on the balcony without rocking back and forth.

Gerald and Amable were at that time reproducing an apparatus, that used to be imported from Paris, that could increase or decrease the size of breasts. The Band Aids were selling, but there was trouble with the workers at the factory, and the government was imposing fines.

They took some time off to establish the old man with a little hobby: A dozen leghorns were purchased and put up on the roof in a compartmentalized cage. Each day they laid one egg a piece, which the old man collected and noted in a notebook.

The dress shop also opened with the two Paris dresses: one real and one fake. Some glossy showcases had been purchased and filled with cheap costume jewelry. So now Mercedes, spent most of the day there with the Bustamante sisters. They had an old Singer treadle machine in the back in which they confected more dresses, getting the patterns right out of their heads.

Then the Band Aids had to be given up. They were broke, and Gerald took a. job with the sugar company. Now he made a laxative for cattle, lumps of raw sugar called *panela*, impotable alcohol, *aguardiente*, and rum—all these being the crude and the less crude products of sugar cane. The impotable alcohol and the aguardiente were bottled in almost identical bottles. She couldn't help thinking of all these products when drinking rum.

By the time El Presidentito was a large toddler, Gerald got a better job with an international food company. He worked on developing a nourishing flour for the poor and they spent a lot of time in their kitchen trying to adapt it to something palatable, substituting it for white flour in biscuit recipes from her wedding gift *Joy of Cooking*. It was all quite dreadful, flat, dry, and fishy, and the *pobres* it was destined for ratified this opinion.

The pounding in the bathroom has stopped and Mrs. Fahey comes in to tell her about the new Sedan de Ville her daughter has ordered in a special color that means she has to wait a month or more for delivery, and to remind her again of the virtues of her grandson with the "photogenic memory."

She, too, has a grandson, thinks Henrietta, and she begins to credit him with qualities she might brag about: his appetite, his avid growing, his curiosity when she told him about San Mateo. She wishes she could tell him all her stories, so that he can connect back. That's what Gerald missed. He couldn't connect back.

And she suspects Jason is like this too. She's sure he never mentions Carol.

XIV

A new participant in Warren's workshop sits off by herself and paints hearts and tulips on wooden plaques. Tole painting, she calls it. Henrietta's heard of it. Troll painting Mike calls it. For sissies, he would say. He and Warren are reliving the Second World War again. Mike was blown up in the Pacific and Warren was in Italy. Sometimes they discuss other wars, the Napoleonic Wars, the Wars of the Roses. Mike watches the History Channel and Warren reads. Henrietta marvels how they keep them all straight. She could never keep more than one war in her head at one time.

Warren gets up and walks around. Suppose you put that tulip over here? he says to the new woman. No, she says, it has to go between the palmetto leaves.

Ah, it's a rule…

Yes. The woman has a thin line of a mouth.

Ah… Troll painting, murmurs Mike.

Warren comes to her, stands behind her painting and grunts perplexity and approval. Then he attacks her sloppy palette, her brushes that should be retired into the trashcan. Her attitude to brushes is like her attitude to favored items of clothing, some of which date back to India and before. The worsted skirt she's wearing she bought from a street vendor in Caracas forty years ago.

Maybe every two years you might invest in a decent brush, Warren says.

Palimpsest, Henrietta says. She has remembered a word she couldn't think of a week ago.

What?

The word I wanted the other day." Unlike matters of more importance, a useless word will always return to her once she leaves off pursuing it and thinks of something else.

Palimp what?

When someone paints over someone else's painting.

A useless bit of information.

You throw me off my stride, he says. I try to talk to you about brushes and…

You know they did a poll in Russia recently, she continues. They had eight hundred thousand replies on little slips of paper stored in bathtubs.

Warren snorts appreciatively. Your kind of people, the Russians.

Once, when we lived in Venezuela, there was an election: the first or second after years of a dictator. The people, of course, were very nervous, didn't go to bed for almost eleven days while they were counting, all by hand. And there were tanks, the end of every street; the worst was they broadcast over loudspeakers up in helicopters: The people should stay calm! The army has no plans for coups of any kind! Imagine it! This voice out of the sky, eleven days...

Jesus!

Listen, do you know who Carlos Castañeda is? she asks.

No idea.

Maybe Priscilla will know, she thinks.

Home at four, she's having creamed chipped beef on toast and frozen baby peas.

When Carol got a little better, due she knows now to the diminishing effects of vincristine, they hugged Henrietta in that group in Mexicali; and Victor and Raul helped them move into the little house they rented on a little street behind the clinic, walking distance to the doctor and the market, and of course her meeting,

It was Raul who found the house, laughably cheap, and cool because it had thick mud walls. It had three whitewashed rooms, a patio with a gallery around with brightly colored railings and doors opening out, smoke blackened kitchen, with a set of vivid plastic dishes on an open shelf, a concrete sink and drainboard, ancient refrigerator, and kerosene stove.

She loved the patio, with its two papaya trees and climbing *veranera* vine, and mossy tile roof that overhung the vine. Where, here and there, she found a crevice or a hole in the *behareque*, she mixed up straw and dung and limewash, which Raul supplied, daubed it on; and Victor came and painted the kitchen and the little parlor, fixed the hinges on the windows, repaired the grills. It was his line of work.

Carol lay in a folding lounge on the east side of the patio in the shade of the *veranera* vine, and drank her carrot and papaya juice, and did some gentle exercises with a woman who came every other day from the clinic, and Henrietta saw their finances, at least, recover.

Every day she shopped, recovering the almost forgotten language of the marketplace; and every day she sat two hours in her meeting, acquiring the flamboyant images of drunkenness and recovery—more like those of a descent into inferno, and assumption into bliss—before the little altar overlooked by Bee Weeson and Doctor Bob. And even the little bell that Victor rang reminded her of days she took the children to the Mass at The Cathedral of Santa Rosa in Milagros.

Whenever I find *those books* open on the floor of Owen's room, I panic... Henrietta reads in Carol's journals.

What books?

Carlos Castañeda was an anthropologist who wrote about some Indians in Mexico that had visions when they ate peyote, Priscilla, finally, tells her one day when she's spooning pap into Adie at The Sunshine Club.

And Charles phones, to make things worse. He needs three hundred dollars to take a course in ultrasound. He has a friend who makes a good living, working nights on weekends only. It will leave him free to hustle the remainder of his time.

Hustle?

You know buy and sell. She doesn't ask what he buys and sells.

And if she'd throw him just another fifty, he could insulate around the wheels of his motor home and maybe he won't freeze his ass off...

Yes, OK. She doesn't want to hear the rest. And it's not as bad as she feared. She'll put the check in the mail tomorrow.

Her heart is doing little somersaults; she goes to lie down. Must take care of myself. She has a little nap, wakes, feeling better.

Must take care of myself. She eats a hardboiled egg with her tea. After that she dials Jason. Owen answers.

I was wondering how you're doing?

OK, I guess. He's not communicative. He's like Mounty, never wanting to answer banal questions, especially on the telephone.

I was thinking maybe we could have another dinner sometime. Nothing formal; maybe just the two of us... Just the blood, speaking to blood, she thinks. He must resent the other child sometimes. There was another, wasn't there? She can't remember sex.

O.K., I guess, he says.

We'll, make it Friday. I'm putting it in my datebook; if your dad can't drop you, let me know, we'll change it, Henrietta says, and thinks now Jason and Sheila can go out, she'll babysit him... Well no, they have the other child. Probably it is Owen who babysits...Ah, well.

He calls her back next day to say he'll come.

At six, she says.

I'll keep it simple, she thinks; and not bring up anything difficult. It's only the start of what will be a long campaign, with no assurance of victory. She shouldn't have been so giddy last week, forgetful of her weakness...of the family weakness.

Friday, Owen's father drops him in the street below. He stops to pet the cat, then picks him up and brings him in.

That's Geoffrey. He's the sixth or seventh marmalade cat I've ever owned, she tells him. He scratches Geoffrey's belly while she broils steaks, and butters baked potatoes, peas...same dinner that he'd liked, but leaving out the aspic. He's silent, so she tells him how she's always had these yellow tigers. Once, when we came here from Venezuela on vacation, leaving the maid to care for one of them. A dog killed it while we were gone, and the maid replaced it with an identical one before we returned and your mother and the others never knew it wasn't the same kitten.

Hmm, he says, face buried in the fur of the cat's flank.

Your medication makes you sleepy? she attempts when they have eaten half the dinner in silence, except for Henrietta's urging food. He lifts his head that's almost lolling in his plate:

Fascist medication, he blurts, too loud. A pea is blown across the table.

What do you mean? she asks. Are all drugs Fascist? She's thinking now of Carlos Castañeda.

No, not all.

Explain it to me. She's had this kind of conversation with Charles, and wonders can she stand another. He's ranting next, about the drugs his friends give him, and on and on, how they are not the same as drugs his enemy..

She only half can listen: Hitler, he shouts and something about a person called don Juan. What can he know of Hitler? she wonders. And what can she know of this Don Juan, whom she assumes is someone out of Carlos Castañeda? She gets up from the table, goes to takes out the chocolate cake she labored over as if it might have some magic, sets a piece before him, takes his plate of uneaten peas.

A path with heart. This phrase she picks out from the rush of bitter jumbled words, and repeats it: Tell me what that means.

He's arrested in his rant by this indication she has listened.

What?

A path with heart. I like it.

Well it's this *don* Juan who said it, seems. Pusher of peyote as she sees him. Tell me what it means to you. I hear you say it several times as if you like it.

I can tell you what it isn't, he says, slightly calmer.

OK.

It isn't the fucking government, and it isn't the Newton Public Schools, and it isn't oh, fuck it...

Please try to tell me.

It isn't doctors. It isn't fascist medication... He can't go on.

She pushes the cake closer to him, and he takes a monstrous bite. His mouth too full of cake to speak, she feels that he may listen if she slips into this breach.

Your mother and I…we were on a path together when we set out for Seattle, then for California. We were looking for a doctor, for a treatment of course you know a little about it…

Doctors… The word strangles him.

Of course, they failed us, the doctors. But they weren't what I thought of when you said a path with heart. I thought of Mexico, where we ended up…

Oh yeah? he gets out, interested most likely due to Carlos Castañeda.

We rented a little adobe house, near the clinic where she went for special essences of fruits and vegetables that came in a powder that we mixed with water from a spring nearby; and when she got a little stronger, she did yoga stretches, and some meditations that a Rebbe had given her, and we gave up thinking where we'd go next, the path was there; it had become no longer an outer but an inner way. And it was a time we talked a lot, and straightened out a lot of things…I wished sometimes you could have been with us, for there were things that had to do with you…

He lifts his head, gives a great swallow. What to do with me? He looks astonishingly like Jason at that moment. Arrests her. Well, someday I'll tell you. You seem angry. So perhaps I'll tell you sometime when you're not…

After he's gone, she thinks it was also something in herself that held her back from telling… The great lies that she paraded: the little adobe house, the vegetables, the talks! It wasn't like that at the end. They weren't together.

Two women alone, more like it…staring at what was coming to each. How will I live? was Henrietta's question; and Carol, how will I die?

She wasn't Carol at the end. One day she was particularly tired, and she said, I've stopped the Taxol. That was the substance from the yew, they'd come so far to try.

Turning me into a frigging man. I'm coming out with whiskers, and my breasts have practically disappeared. Henrietta nodded. She'd seen it happening if she could admit it.

Neither mentioned going any farther. It had become an interior path. That part at least was true.

It never occurred to her then that Carol, in addition to being terribly ill, was far more alone than she. She had Victor and Raul and all the others; she could go out to the market, chatter about the ripeness of the pineapples and the sweetness of the melons. But Carol, who could chatter in Spanish long ago—

she had been small when they'd moved on to India—had lost the language. They had left behind her women's groups, her dancer friends.

I should have thought of that. I should have tried to get her back, at least to California. I was wrapped up in myself. How would I live, and who would love me now? That was all I thought about.

You were human...

Who said that once? She can't remember. Thinks it must have been that woman, touched her arm once in the basement of the Baptist...Yes, her son died, someone... I must find her! A path with heart. There must be something in him, Owen, if I can bear to tease it out. He seems to her at this moment a great tangle of string, of knitting worsted, that will take an eternity to sort out.

Don't worry about it. Give him back.

A great sob escapes her. Carol told her how, on the worst occasions—one night when Owen began having strange friends and didn't come home for two days—she'd recalled the contract she was under, the gift she must, like Hannah, give back. It was the contract all of us are under, for that matter. We all have to give our children back.

She'll tell him. On another occasion. Must go easy on myself, she thinks. I'm weak. I suffer from the Korsakoffs, and things that would be easy for another aren't so easy.

Then she remembers a name. Lucy. Lucy is the one who said that about her being human. Sat next to me and talked about her son-in-law who died.

Sometimes it seems her memory is coming back. They tell her the results from the little quizzes they give her periodically show she is no better; no worse, but no better.

She thinks she'd arranged to see Owen again, another dinner party, a series of dinner parties: every second Friday, they'd decided. Did this really happen? Yes, it's in her notebook. There'd be more occasions. She steadies herself. I'll do better. Blood to blood. All those parties she gave to strangers. Blood to blood, and it will take a while. Many dinners.

So hard to tell the truth. I've spent a half a century embroidering the truth, she says in women's step meeting she goes to in the basement of the Methodist church on Moody Street. It happens before I know it, all the time. And Lucy, who is seated opposite her at the table, nods. She's found her. Quite a feat. She has to be a kind of sleuth to ascertain the simplest matters. I remember when I was having blackouts, she goes on. They called them mental lakes, the group in Mexicali. Anyhow, I woke one morning, called the operator on the phone to ask what day it was. We're not allowed to give that information, she told me.

Laughter. Women's laughter. Oh, if God can have his jokes, well women have a joke or two. They're sitting on baby chairs around a baby table. Above them is a chart with stars for Sunday School attendance. The chairs are difficult for Henrietta's stiffened legs. It's chairs that she remembered and associated with Lucy that brought her back to this meeting she'd forgotten to go to lately.

We're such lucky people, Lucy says when it's her turn. Why anything could have caused us to miss this life. The smallest thing. A couple of brain cells damaged more'n we already have. A stupid reason to walk out and not come back... I can remember sitting in my first meeting and the basket's passed to me, and I think so this's what they want from me, my money! Well this nicest man that's sitting beside me, says, My dear, if you don't have it you don't have to put it in. How did he know? How did he know I'm thinking of running out of there...?

I thought about you, Henrietta says to Lucy after the meeting. Talk about the brain cells. If I'd had one more damaged, I couldn't have remembered... where I see you. Or remembered what you said once.

Lucy hugs her: What did I say?

I couldn't tell you at the moment, Henrietta says, but it helped me at the moment.

She gets home and finds a Letter from Kate in the hall mail drop. Oh Dear God; she doesn't open it until she goes upstairs and settles herself with tea and a pastry she's brought home from the meeting.

Dear Mother (Kate always called her Mother, unlike the others. Motherrr. Carol called her Ma.)

Uncle Mounty loaned me 4 thou, so I could take a course and update my nursing license. Which I've already started and hope to finish in a month.

He said he had to let you know he'd heard from you, which I didn't want him to do, but anyway, here's some of my life that you missed.

I married a very wealthy man when I was twenty three. We had two children and bought a beautiful house in Webster—not too far from Uncle Mounty. It has 5 bedrooms, a stone fireplace, hardwood floors, and a barn...

Henrietta reads this far and has to put the letter (3pages) in her notebook, closes her eyes and takes deep breaths, telling herself that the girl must be all right; she's taking a course, doesn't seem to need her Motherr right now...

Just let her be mad at me. Don't let her need me, she importunes her Higher Power.

Just let me stop there and read the rest later. There's no return address, she notes. Maybe this can be taken in little by little, and I can go on being happy...

XV

Palimpest, eh? says Warren, who's spreading a coat of burnt sienna over another of the canvases destined for the dumpster.

Palimp sest, Henrietta corrects him.

A naive painter isn't supposed to know so many fancy words, says Mike.

That's right, says Warren. Don't be getting above yourself there madam.

...means a painting over another painting." she says. It's things like this I can occasionally remember, nothing useful.

They have a model today, a young man, Skip, who's wearing a dhoti he got in India, sitting on a brocade curtain in lotus position. She paints a river at the bottom of her canvas, and across the river a city's arches and domes, then the sky, a brilliant cerulean. The brocade curtain, she causes to float in the sky, like a carpet, and on it Skip floats, crosslegged, a little smile on his face.

He works as a nurse in the State Hospital. Once a year he goes to India for a month to meditate. He's absented himself right now. It's why she paints him up there. His body is sensual, almost sexless, rounded like a woman's and he's tanned to a warm apricot tone. His sex is partly visible, a small animal curled up in the pubic fur. He wouldn't be embarrassed if he knew this; he usually poses nude at Brandeis.

They aren't real art students here. Henrietta knows nothing of anatomy, and she's got the legs all wrong. Mike struggles, but it's not really his kind of subject and the Tole painter has turned with disgust back to her tulips and hearts.

Did you know your jewels are on view? Mike says.

Oh, yeah, Skip shrugs. He lives comfortably in two worlds. When he goes to work at the hospital, he tucks his long beard into his shirt. Only the painters he poses for know he has it. Henrietta is accustomed to bits of skin and intimate parts glimpsed through saris and dhotis.

Better on view than hidden away, she says. She remembers a year when they lived in Venezuela—it was the same year the astronauts went to the moon—they went up into the mountains to try to buy some silver jewelry from the indigenous people. They didn't see a single strand or bead. Just dark hovels with people huddled under blankets around a fire and a cook pot. She thought about the astronauts on the moon and had a sense of intense dislocation. Later, they learned the jewelry was hidden under the layers of blankets.

To live in two worlds at once.

It was a thing most people never tried, or wanted to. It helped to have a golden body like Skip's. She had always been intensely aware of her whiteness, her cold northern eyes, when she'd lived among southern people.

Carol had no one but me, thinks Henrietta, stumping home with her canes, her painting in a pack on her back; and it was natural we got on one another's nerves, especially as she weakened, and I had to take on more; our ratios of energy were skewed: since Carol was a child, almost, she'd been stronger, seeing into Henrietta's fraudulence, and making up her lacks.

Each evening then, when the heat began to lift and a breeze began to stir the leaves of the veranera vine and flap the oilcloth on the patio table they used for all their meals, they rose from their reclining chairs and, arms linked—she tried to make it seem from comradeship and not because of Carol's weakness— they walked along the broken sidewalk to the corner, where the little grocer displayed his cheeses and his plantains to the flies, and down the Avenida Guadalupe toward the river where the day girl they had hired took their clothes to wash; then, turning at the foot of hill, they walked past some attractive older houses with entryways lined in painted tiles and seductive, shuttered windows.

They sometimes had to stop, midblock, for Carol to take a series of deep rattling breaths—the cancer had probably returned to what was left of her right lung—and at the turn, where they could walk the half block to their door, she'd sometimes say, I'll walk a little higher here. And they would pass under some acacia trees that fronted a girls' academy, and Carol would finger a leaf, or stare at a flower, say, how odd. Or, isn't that a strange color to the sky, or look at the funny shape, that cloud, or there's another one of those stray horses, or look at the pretty legs on that dirty little girl, not really expecting an answer from Henrietta, simply wondering at the world.

And once she looked into her mother's eyes and said, I'm sorry, I'm really sorry; and that statement, also, seemed to require no reply. Only sorrow. It was the kind of sorrow Henrietta used to feel when her children—especially Charles—confronted her with questions like that one she'd shocked Lutie with, in the bath that time. The birds and the bees, the facts of life, and matters like the food chain and the death of stars. It isn't my universe, you know, she wanted to tell them. To me it's an embarrassment.

And every day or two some beauty that had been Carol's was dulled. Her hair had lost its thickness since the Cytoxin; and now it seemed to lose its life, its spring; her skin was dry, developed creases. How hard it must be to love a child born without beauty. She recalled how all of hers had laid this early claim on her by unexpected handsomeness and grace. Especially Carol. As she grew, she made you think of Jesus' statement about those who *have*, having all manner of good things added.

But once the cancer entered it became the other way around: those who have little shall have even that little taken... She doesn't often think of Jesus, but will admit that he was shrewd. Yes shrewd and humorless. Well what was so funny anyway? Had Carol read the New Testament as part of her reading program? she asked her once. No, she was too weary after the Old.

All Henrietta can remember from all her sitting in every Sunday school basement in West Boylston as a child, is a vague idea of where to locate the Sea of Galilee and the Jordan River. And of course some parables, and the Christmas story, which had never had the slightest power to move her; This year being no exception as she watches its plaster representatives being lifted out of excelsior placed on the Common. Oh it makes her weary; they bring it all out earlier every year, bypassing even that other obligatory festivity coming in two weeks.

XVI

The first Irish nurse grasps her shoulders, while the second lifts, pushes, pulls her right leg, holding at the ankle.

We'll have you dancing, says first.

We'll have you kickin' up your heels.

That will be delightful, Henrietta says. Do many people get...this better, as I have?

Ah, no, we think you are a lovely exception to the rule, we do, says the red haired one, tickling her, and then allowing her to sit.

Now if you'll step up on this walking machine and walk your daily quarter of a mile, dear.

Make it more, she says.

Well one more quarter, says the dark one. We make it anymore we'll have to send you for another electrocardiogram, you see.

But why? Is something wrong...my heart?

Oh, that's not our department, dearie.

But is it just routine, or did they say it 'specially in my case?

Oh, just routine.

Ridiculous; but she's relieved; is she become like Megan, wanting to stick around to see how things turn out? Well, yes, she thinks, I do.

No cane, all weekend about the house without it though she uses it to go to the meeting down the street on Saturday night, and to the Congregational Church down town on the bus.

She feels so full of herself and her new vigor Sunday afternoon, that she takes out the letter. And skims the second page for any words like "cancer" or 'detox". Finds none but notes the word "schizophrenia", reads this section closely with flutters in her heart.

But it's not blood; it's the rich husband who's been thrown out of the house with 5 bedrooms, stone fireplace... and put in an institution.

Not blood. Thank God! What does she care about the rich fool married her daughter?

She, Kate, needs to go back to nursing to be able to stay in the big house, Henrietta ascertains by closely reading one just that one part of the letter with the toxic word.

Not her responsibility, the poor man. Kate always thought she could straighten out any boy that came along. A good lesson for her.

She puts the letter away for another time. If it weren't stuck in her notebook she'd probably forget it entirely. Light of foot, she goes about the kitchen making soup to warm the kitchen. It was down below ten degrees this week in November.

The next time Mrs Fahey boasts about her granddaughter,s photogenic memory, and her daughter's Coup de Ville, she might boast about her Kate's house with stone fireplace with barn and 5 bedrooms…

She makes the same dinner again for Owen, using her notebook to remind her. Jason drops him off and he comes up the stairs with the cat in his arms and carries him to the couch to tease him while she sets things out. Again he eats hungrily and asks for seconds, reminding her of Charles when he was growing.

I like giving dinner parties for you. You know why, she says.

He shakes his head but looks up from his plate.

Because you're good and hungry. When I used to have big parties in Venezuela, some people didn't even eat. They had a buzz on from the drinks and didn't want to lose it by eating.

Your grandma included, she adds.

He laughs, which delights her. Blood calling to blood

This time he seems to be happy just hearing her talk, so she gets out the other album, the one from Venezuela.

The first pictures she has trouble recalling. Some lichen stained low white buildings, looming mountains behind. Oh, here's Charles standing by the monkey cage…

This was the day after we arrived. We went out to see the sights while we were still living in a hotel. It was a private zoo left over from the days of a legendary dictator. He had fathered hundreds of children it was said. And most of the property in this small city was still owned by the one wife he acknowledged, who was still living there. An illiterate Indian, people believed he had magic powers. Whenever the thought of assassinating him entered the heads of any of his officers, he knew it and had them assassinated.

He moved the capital there from Caracas, but it moved back after he died. They said a rhinoceros that lived in that zoo would only come out of its mud pond if he called it. Now it never came out. But I watched an elephant eating cigarette butts from the pavement and no one to stop them, or clean up, and the monkeys…a very derelict place.

And do you know monkeys are just like children? They need toys!

Here's the one, a gibbon I think, she finds the photo. He studied me just as carefully as I studied him. And then, I got too close, and he found a toy within his reach…my glasses.

Wow, says Owen. I would have brought them a box of toys.

That's exactly what I did. A week or so later—I was driving around blind till I got another pair of glasses made up. And, when I went back, he wasn't there.

Why not?

Well, when a guard of some sort finally showed up. He said the gibbon died. He ate something… And I remembered how after he had studied my glasses from every angle and even seemed to…

To try them on?

Yes, actually. I remember that pretty clearly.

But why didn't you try to take them back?

I don't know…

You should have.

But I didn't. We were screaming for someone to help us.

You should have just reached in and taken them.

I guess so. I'm sorry I didn't because I did see him breaking them into pieces and putting them in his mouth like a two-year old.

Oh gramma!

I'm sorry. Can you forgive me?

He doesn't answer, burying his face in Geoffrey's fur.

It was long ago…

And did you at least give the toys to the other monkeys?

I really can't remember…

Why can't you?

Well, I had this buzz on for twenty years. It's a wonder I even remember this poor gibbon.

She hopes for another conspiratorial laugh here, but gets more silence.

Sometimes I wish I could be a cat, Owen confides to Geoffrey. Or a dog, or a wolf, he says into Geoffrey's fur.

And Henrietta is carried back in that rented house on Route 62, when a cat died in her early months of sobriety and then two birds, feet upturned in the bottom of the cage, and then the lovely dog was hit by a car.

After he leaves, shaking her hand, no kiss, she has a few bad moments about her relations to the animal world, and tries to feel the pain of that gibbon crunching up and swallowing her lenses, made of glass back then. O Dear…

She makes some chamomile tea then and eats the left over potato skins with some lovely butter. Just as she's about to sit down, Geoffrey meows at her as she's forgotten to feed him.

Oh you stupid cat, she says, getting up to open one of the little cans of his current favorite.

Then she sits down again to her tea and forgives herself. Stupid monkey. By trying on the glasses he gave her a false sense of his intelligence. Who would have thought he might want to eat a pair of glasses!

The world hurts Owen the way it used to hurt Charles, she thinks. But he's a kind boy, she thinks. And has some ideals. Maybe the world will be kind till he's stronger. But what can she do?

She wonders if more of the photos in the album carry these harsh messages. She puts the photo of the ruin of San Mateo which had fallen out back in its proper place. She'll have to stick to the ones with humans in them to be safe. That will be easy because Gerald would never take a photo without at least one of his relatives in it.

Sheila has invited her to Newton for Thanksgiving. That is nice. She likes Sheila.

XVII

Dot Slamin Hill's American Legion Band is marching down Moody Street, and a little group from Sunshine Club has walked to the corner to see them tootle by: Dot Hill with pumping arm and bobbing shako in her thirtieth year of marching and of widowhood. She's no intention of quitting, says the *News Trib*. And if they win the competition this year they'll go to Russia.

Bobby Rosier and Berta Bechtel give a salute as they march by, and Adie bangs her spoon on the tray of the geriatric chair she's fastened into. The snow has all melted, and it's warm as April again. When they get back and go inside Rebecca sets them to making paper chains to hang in the windows.

Henrietta notes that Megan's absent. Becca doesn't know what happened; but Priscilla tells her, when she sees her at the Service Center after, that Megan's had another stroke, is in the Waltham Hospital, not expected to recover fully. What if she's taken like her sisters? Henrietta wonders.

Well, it will be awful, says Priscilla. But she wouldn't be aware...

Yes, that's the awful part. Henrietta recalls the dreadful things Megan's said and thought about her sisters, thinks it should be required in a life to be aware when a similar fate comes round to one, to make some kind of connection... But perhaps it's too painful.

Priscilla shrugs. The way life is. It's why I toy around with the idea of reincarnation. That way Megan's task, the next time round, will be to figure out this horror.

Well, I suppose; but God is merciful. Another way to look at it.

Oh Megan! she thinks. She's sure there are scientists and all who worry... about the Universe in preference to their stomachs or the latest gossip; but Megan was the only one she'd ever been acquainted with who worried about Creation in that way...

I'll miss her terribly, Priscilla says. It's only dawning on me now, how much.

Of course. You read to her...

I think we must have read her that book on Mozart four times.

The three of them used to want to live until the Big Bang theory was proved or disproved, then only Megan. Now she'll be like Winnie, remembering only words out of the books; or, like Adie, remembering only her baby days.

A couple days later, Becca takes small group, to visit Megan; it's the custom in the Sunshine Club when someone's in the hospital, Henrietta is included. But six people standing round her bed is not a good idea in Megan's case. They try to say they miss her, true in only Henrietta's case she fears, lean close to hear what she is saying;

The Virgin Mary, it sounds like. The Virgin Mary is offended? Can it be? If it is, it's troubling her mightily, and the little group is told to leave their handmade cards on the table, and file out as quick as possible.

The Virgin Mary, among others, certainly ought to be offended by Megan.

But how cruel! The religion of Megan's childhood, cast off as thoroughly as is possible, come back to torment her!

When Gerald had his first other woman, she's pretty sure it was the first, it was, oddly enough, a woman who reminded her of herself. Janie. She and Janie were close friends in those days that they rented the house in New England and Gerald had some training for his new post in India. They sold the house in Pance and flew in a jet this time, very high and very fast above the clouds that hid the blue green Caribbean. She had three children with her, who would eat nothing but the sugars and the creamers and the little envelopes of salad dressing off their trays; and she needed to sedate herself with martinis, so that she didn't experience, this time, the exaltation of altitude or the hopeful unrolling of her life before her.

Janie was at the airport with her husband to meet them and to introduce them to the house she had rented for them. That house that was filled in all its recesses with the previous life of its owners. They seemed to have saved every tire they ever owned and every exam paper their daughter ever wrote, giggled Janie, showing her the family portraits hanging behind the oil burner.

The new company explained some of what happened. There were parties every weekend. The couples did everything together. She looked back with nostalgia at the days of the Band Aid factory in Barrio Pinchinche, the Harold Lloyd assembly line creaking around the old barn, and Charles sleeping in his basket in the shade of a silkcotton tree.

There were so many parties, it seemed like all one party when she looks back. There had been parties in Maracay of course, and she had begun to discover two things already: one, that she could be vastly entertaining when she tried; and two, that she preferred the odd guests—the bearded Peace Corps volunteer, the slightly suspect journalist, the graduate student investigating forest myths—to the important people who ran the companies and whom Gerald expected her to cultivate, and whom she perversely decided to dislike. The higher up they were, the more she disliked them.

These new parties included only the latter. A few of the men were liberally educated and interesting, so she engaged them on men's topics, refusing to be left with the women on the corner sofa or in the kitchen. She and Janie ranged the room, scorning their business talk and making fun of them. The war engaged them. Janie opposed the war, and Henrietta interested herself in this new conflict, not the one that Gerald had carefully avoided—though he said later it had left him somehow incomplete that he never went.

It was a performance that couldn't be sustained, however, because by the end of every party she entered a state where she seemed to hold up her end but could never remember, the next morning, that final part of the evening. She took refuge in frequent illness. She had many interesting ailments at that time and brought them to many doctors, who were completely baffled, though they seemed to find her symptoms interesting and did many tests.

Her old home, New England, shocked her with its rains that lasted for weeks not hours and or parts of a day as in Maracay. She couldn't accept again the dark that came in the middle of the afternoon, these serious seasons that reflected the creaking over of the whole tremendous machinery, not some eddy of clouds come over the *cordillera*.

The dark afternoons made her sad and heedless of the moody children. The war, too, was an animus picked up by the women and children that made the world somber; and it had one large benefit that she seized in her lethargy, allowing her hair to uncurl and throwing out her heels and pantyhose.

Janie sat in her kitchen, and their lives struck them funny as they sipped vermouth, a drink that was allowed women in the middle of the afternoon in Pinchinche, she told Janie.

This place of pale and subtle flora, austere in winter, like the high *cordillera*, accorded with her true nature, she thought; and this return brought out a childish stubbornness. So when she found out that Janie's husband had moved in with his secretary and that Gerald was visiting Janie to put in her storm doors and to comfort her in ways that necessitated carrying the condoms he supplied himself with to thwart her own carelessness with contraceptives.

She actually left him for several months, rented herself an apartment in and old brick building near what had been an old lace mill in the center of their little town.

She stopped drinking quite so much, and actually found herself a job as a taxi dispatcher at night. Her fancy education prepared her for nothing better. She put the children in a school filled with Portuguese and rode a bicycle.

Gerald came and repaired things, and one day when he was under the sink seeing to a leak, desire rose in her to such an degree that they went in the bedroom and he made her pregnant—she became pregnant whenever she wished in those days.

And so the experiment was over. She took up her afternoon vermouth again, without Janie, and within a few months, they were in India and right after that Carol was born.

And those were the worst years. She barely remembers them. There was a servant, Benita, who dealt with the children, and two went away to a school in England and finally they were back here again.

Albany, New York had been the place where Gerald ended up. He ran a plant in Troy that made tomato paste, supposedly until retirement. She left him again during this time, when she found out he was having another desultory friendship with a woman in the personnel department.

First, she'd lived with Charles, who had dropped out of high school and seemed content to spend the rest of his life on the sofa, and with Carol who was still in elementary school. The other two lived with Gerald, by their choice. She rented an old bungalow with a big yard, and had a beagle they all loved, and two yellow tabby cats—Mono the Eighth and Mono the Ninth, as well as a guinea pig and two parakeets. She was drunk by two every afternoon, and it was Carol who took care of the house and Charles.

It was funny, the things you concentrated on when pain was everywhere. She remembers it was the animals. They all seemed doomed to tragedies. First the guinea pig escaped and lived furtively in the corners of the house, like a rat, subsisting on the seeds the parakeets dropped, and flitting across the floor late at night like a blond rat when she got up to the bathroom. Then she found the two birds on their backs at the bottom of the cage. This seemed to her worse than the waste of Charles's life. Then, the cat run over on the highway, and Carol having to bury him while Henrietta was in the hospital with one of her mystery illnesses.

But the worst was the dog; the lovely beagle with the liquid eyes was run over on the same busy road where the Mono had been killed.

She had no street sense, that dog that she called Rumple and the children called Puppy. When Gerald came to visit, he brought her a can of dog food, as if she, Henrietta Rose, couldn't provide for anyone, not even a dog. He called her Pooch, and noted how they couldn't even name a dog together.

Her leg was shattered, and she nearly died. She took the money from a house settlement that was to last them years and spent it all on the dog. She was so easy to love, a Beagle mix with liquid eyes. They pinned the bone and they brought her home high on morphine.

She didn't know then that a dog with a pinned leg is always in pain. They ought to have taken it off, for all it was any use to her. She dragged it behind her when she set off after squirrels. They were supposed to exercise the leg in warm baths, but Henrietta had no resources to do anything further.

For all was pain. The house was full of pain. That child who had opened her womb, whose limbs had beaten against her heartfloor, was listening to voices. His eyes were glittering and hard. The furniture in his room was upside down, and he went in and out through the upper windows instead of the front door, jumping off the roof to chase the school bus. The beagle was frightened of him too and practically lived with the Chilean refugees next door.

And Carol found him one day clutching the yellow cat around the neck. A voice had told him to strangle it. A doctor, who had told her Charles was simply undergoing a difficult adolescence, suddenly paid attention and sent him to the state hospital the only place where you could go if you protested, and Charles always protested. At the local hospital they had the docile patients who took their meds and sat in a nice lounge. Charles walked out of there at the first opportunity the two times he was there.

They put him in a room with a bare mattress and a pail to pee in, she remembers. The second day, they let her in. She found him nude and clutching an asbestos blanket. She sat beside him silently and noted the cherry colored mole above his backside she hadn't seen for fifteen years.

And that was just at the same time the beagle with the liquid eyes walked outside in the deep snow and rebroke the leg. Henrietta failed to notice the bone protruding, and left her unattended while she attended to Charles; and by the time she noticed the dog she was having trouble breathing, and when they got her to the vet she was barely living. I can't afford to save her this time, Henrietta told the vet. She was numb to suffering by then. And so the doctor gave the injection and she held the dog, thinking there'd be time for a soft word before she was gone, but the liquid eyes were frozen by the time she put her face to the soft muzzle.

Happens in a split second, said the vet.

She isn't prepared to walk into the house in Newton, which Carol had never lived in, but which contained a green sofa Henrietta did recall from that other house where Owen was born, and where she'd made a stab at being a help to a young mother. A rocking chair in front of fireplace, she remembered also; it came from West Boylston, had rocked many Montague babies before Owen. Carol used to keep it in the bedroom. And there were things Henrietta had kept from travels, and had given to Carol when she married: framed *mola* from Colombia, depicting a set of water birds; sausage shaped baskets from the Amazon, that they used to kneed the yucca root, hung either side of the bookshelf. She couldn't look at the bookshelf, knowing it was full of Carol's books. Across the top was a bright woven runner of the kind the peasants would walk from Ecuador over the border to sell on sidewalks.

You'll have a drink? says Sheila. Oh no, I'm sorry, I forgot. I have some...

Juice is fine. She sinks into the green sofa, at its mercy. Owen, not disposed to rescue her, is teasing Sheila's child, a well-fed girl with long dark hair, who's sitting in an armchair with her feet stuck out and staring at Henrietta. I didn't know you had a grandma too, she says to Owen.

Oh, God! says Owen, who's leaning over back of the child's chair and threatening to tip it backwards.

I have two grandmas, says the girl. One, we're going to see at five o'clock. We have to eat another dinner.

Oh, you think that you can fit it...? says Owen. The child is rather fat actually.

In my stummick, sure. She pats her ample middle.

She's a pig, says Owen; then he's bored and goes away. She thinks his face is pasty today, his hair, so golden as a baby, was lank and dull.

I told you to wash your face, his father calls after in a tone that says he knows Owen won't. They were more festive at their dinner yesterday at the Sunshine Club, she thinks. This is one of those new ruptured and rejoined families that the sitcoms have it are so rollicking and hilarious.

Of course the old families weren't much better. She recalls the year she disappointed Lutie, still alive at time, refusing to attend a family Christmas. She spent it at an Alcathon in Troy—a kind of all night marathon of meetings—and she remembers being grateful that they hadn't managed even a Christmas tree or the slightest reminder of the holiday in that church basement.

In those early days of Alcathons, you got giddy from the coffee, from two sleepless nights if you could manage it. She did. She and Peggy K.—where is she now?—lay wrapped in coats on the pewlike benches that lined the walls and laughed all night at nothing. A mistake, she thinks, this elbowing my way back into a family. What was I thinking of? Well out of it as I've been, for three years now. Except for Charles.

Charles still comes to her on Christmas, takes her to the midnight service at The First Congregational Church, accepts a generous check that barely comes in time to save him from whatever latest difficulty he's gotten into.

She'll have to write him soon, renew the rite...

They sit down to eat and Sheila loads the plates with turkey at one end, asking if people want white or dark. The other dishes they pass around. It's all nicely prepared, even fresh mashed potatoes, as well as baked sweet potatoes.

I'm sick, says Owen halfway through, and leaves the table. Everything is very nice, she hastens to tell Sheila, who looks harried. She feels sick herself, but eats the perfectly decent dinner, helps clean up, amazed as always how much longer the cleaning up takes than the eating.

No reminders of the former house in the kitchen; she can have a fellow feeling for the female working beside her: intelligent and efficient with the leftovers, grateful for employment and for company. In fact, as Sheila is rinsing and Henrietta is loading the dishwasher, Sheila comes close to admitting it's not working out with Jason.

He acted like a shit to Carol, but he was afraid, says Henrietta tentatively.

He's going to abandon Owen, too, I see it coming, Sheila says.

And you?

Well I'm more likely than his father to stick by him, Sheila says, misunderstanding Henrietta's meaning. Jason thinks that if a kid has lots of toys and a nice house and the school system's good, it is enough.

Ah, yes...

It's why I'm glad you're in the picture, says Sheila.

Oh dear, oh dear... But what I meant by my question is will he stick by you?

More likely I'll leave him. We haven't married. I had an advantageous settlement from my former...

Ah. So, she's free. We're all free in the eyes of everybody but our children. She recalls the eyes of the fat child in the armchair. She'll exact her due, yes, later if not sooner.

Well, it's only one day in the year. The sun is going down behind the wintery trees outside the kitchen window; Jason, ignorant probably of any coming troubles, is winding a scarf around his neck and stamping in his hiking boots preparatory to dropping her off on their way to another grandmother.

One thing I do believe, says Sheila in a voice that's meant for Jason to hear. When Owen says he's sick and leaves the table like that, he really is; I went in once and checked on him; his hands were clammy and his face had beads of sweat...

Well I sincerely doubt it, Jason says. Let's go. And they all troop back to his

Volvo in the detached garage and pile in, Owen pale and silent in the front with his father.

She makes a cup of tea, sits at her kitchen table and reads the skimpy holiday edition of The Globe. There is no news, won't be for three more days. The world has stopped till Monday—no mail, no banks, no Sunshine Club—affording all these merged and shuffled families time to get around to all the grandmothers.

Geoffrey still looks offended, so she talks to him sweetly and tells him she's sorry. Why is she sorry? She forgets. Checks her pocketbook where she always puts creamers for him, finds the little packet of turkey she brought back from Jason's.

Why is she sorry? She can't recall, but tries to investigate the vague feeling. According to the notebook, she had the nice dream again: Lutie this time coaxing her up the soft green hill, then Lutie changes to someone else, she didn't write it down.

Certainly it isn't a good idea to follow Lutie. She must think about this.

"Called Geoffrey a stupid cat," she reads in her notebook. Can that be it? "Owen reminds me of Charles as little boy, too sensitive, a spoiled idealist he became…"

Oh dear I hope not!

But what can she do about it? About anything?

"Becca's quiz says I should grow up to be a cruise director," she reads on a previous page. Followed by: "Out of the whole Reality Orientation miserable company I'm only one with poss of growing up."

Ha!

DINNERPARTIES! This in Caps.

"BLOOD speak to blo…" Well, I can do that. I am doing that.

Charles calls. What are you doing? she asks him.

Well, I'm shivering in a phone booth. What did you expect?

Ah, well then I'll have to say I appreciate your call. I'm trying to think of today as just another day.

Oh, yeah, me too.

So no one has invited him, she thinks.

I went to Jason's for dinner. He has a new woman, very nice.

Oh, well, he says, I have this deal. Some building materials I'm trying to move. I wondered if you wanted to invest…

No thanks. I sent you up a hundred.

Ah yes, I would've invested that except I needed it to keep from starving.

Of course, that's why I sent it. She hears coins falling, wonders if he'll want to…

Take the number; call me back, he shouts.

I'll have to get a pencil.

Hurry.

But the line is disconnected. She waits for the ring, the angry voice. Is there a time that he's not angry?

It comes. Will she accept the call from…

Yes, of course.

It's cheaper if you call me back. I try to save you a little money, he complains.

Never mind. I'll have to hang a pencil round my neck... Or maybe if she hung a tape recorder, sort of an auxiliary to a faulty brain...she thinks while he is telling her about the missed opportunity to double her money. She wonders if Mounty might take this nephew in, and they could wheel and deal together. Did you ever think of going into business with your Uncle Mounty? It would be a place to...

That booze hound! He yelps.

...a place to live, to...

Charles never drank, preferring hallucinogens. A year ago he told her he had quit. Got scared of them, in her opinion.

But he'd forgotten, it seemed, how to live. At least like other people.

Forget it. You're not taking up the booze again, I hope. He says this with a trace of affection that makes her want to cry.

Of course not. Are you crazy? Throw away seven years!

He will not go to any program. Everything, he does alone. All his life, since babyhood, he's been like that. Once, when he was barely seven, Gerald absentmindedly dropped him at a boyfriend's house in a strange neighborhood miles from where they lived in Maracay, drove off without observing that no one answered the door. Charles took the better part of day in finding his way home. It was his grandest hour, she believes. I am his only friend, she thinks; she tells him that she loves him, and expects him Christmas. It was what he called about, in spite of not even mentioning it. He knows by now that she's not likely to sink money into any project other than to keep him reasonably warm and fed.

Tom at ten

How nice, to get back to routine. And only Christmas left to stumble through.

But she has plans this year. A dinner in the manner of her days as gracious hostess of the North American Communities of Maracay and Ranpore. She counts her chairs with satisfaction; not enough, even with Jason's contribution. She hopes today that Tom will take her to the storage vault in Natick, help her dig out some more of her own chairs and the leaf to the table. She has hinted that she'll pay him well.

She sits in the Loony Noony plotting it all out.

She'll invite, Mounty; he must come; and Owen, Jason, Sheila, her daughter—she forgets her name—and Charles, and me...that's six, no seven. She calculates the size of the table leaf she hasn't seen for fifteen years, since Gerald died.

Pat O is speaking, one of the oldtimers:

...used to hang around with Boonie Pooler, Jimmy Lynch. Jimmy Lynch the rag and bone man. Don't give a hang for any man! We called ourselves the Bleachery Boys, and rode around together in Jimmy's wagon, tipping up the bottle frequently enough, we three.

The dogs would follow, grab our ankles. Who's dog is that? we'd make inquiry. If no one would own up to it, we'd stab it dead, and then the owner would show up as sure as Sunday comes; what could he say? We made inquiries, ha ha.

In those days the Irish would come in your house and sing and dance. They called them Kitchen Rackets. French came too, Acadians. We, neither of us, French or Irish, would ever forgive the British. We'd drink to that, and understand each other. I had a friend named Herve le Blanc that could outswill an Irishman...

I'll have a ham, she thinks. It's easier than a turkey. Or a leg of pork. She had a cook who used to simmer it in beer and orange juice, scallions and cilantro.

You and your dinner parties, she scolds herself. What good are they? I might be active in the union movement, or harangue for peace, something, like that girl, Priscilla, does some good to someone...

She used to feel the same about the Peace Corp people, she would meet sometimes at parties. She would plan to run away from Gerald, go to them and ask if she could help: She'd dig a well, or hoe some vegetables...yes, desert her children too of course.

Carol had inherited some of these propensities; she wanted Jason to go out to Africa and teach with her that year she had the fellowship. He wouldn't. Was that when their problems started? She, herself, was drinking, at her worst those years. A wonder she remembers any of it. Listen, she tells herself. You are here to listen.

She always likes to hear Pat. One of the poets of sobriety, she thinks of him: ...wouldn't call them wasted years, he's saying. We had a lot of fun. We did. But then I started getting sick. I blamed it on too many screwdrivers, the orange juice, must've been, I thought; it couldn't've been the other. And getting old. They take my picture at the registry; I hand it back to them: this ain't me.

Scared me, that, that face on my driver's license. I scurried after you fellows awhile, got six months or so... And then I felt so good, I gave myself a treat, I went to Ireland, had a monumental drunk. You only need to breathe in Ireland, and you're lost.

Here I'd almost convinced myself I could stay sober and go to Ireland, twice a year and have meself a fling, ho ho... It was eighteen months before I could get meself back to you dear people.

Ha ha! The lies we tell ourselves. I pray, for honesty every day, just like I brush my teeth. You don't find out the benefits at first. It's only when you see the dentist.

One month, one day, and fifteen minutes sober, Tom announces early next morning. She creeps down. His pickup's held together now with bumper stickers: on doors, and hood, and fenders, everywhere. A conversation piece; she hopes its insides hold together for the twenty miles or so to Natick.

The leaf is larger than she thought, and then she finds the peeled sapling in a pot of gravel she has used as a Christmas tree ever since her first Christmas in Santa Rita, and the box of tin birds, and the papier mache apples to hang on it. It used to be a conversation piece at her parties. And there are two small chairs. Two more people will fit. Would Tom? Well that is if he's free on Christmas...

Oh, sure, he says. I'm always free. He's left behind, he tells her, seven kids, two wives, two businesses. Cleaned out, he tells her, taking both hands off the wheel and spreading his fingers while the pickup veers across the mid-line of Route Nine, and chairs and leaf jolt up and down behind them.

I tell myself every morning: no relationships the first year. Every time I see a girl that looks good to me, I make myself remember all my marriages one by one. Remember how, for every one I had, I had to kick and bite and wrestle myself away from it, like a dog fighting for a bone, Jesus...

Well I exaggerate, I guess. I have a little girl was born with only half an arm. Someday I'll have to think about it.

Of course, you will; not now.

Yeah. Easy Does It, One Day At a Time, all that.

Yes, thinks Henrietta. Like his truck, his life is held together by these bumper stickers.

He comes in with her, helps her put the leaf in; it makes the kitchen crowded; so they drag the table into the living room, and rearrange the chairs and lamps. The table, of panama mahogany made to order in Maracay, has always been too lovely for a kitchen. She runs her hands over it and finds the spot where a macaw they used to own took a bite out of it one day when he got down out of his ring among the giant philodendrons of the patio.

This furniture marks a great change in her life she thinks. Up until now, she's purposely kept the furniture to a minimum, assuming she'd get back on the train someday, continue her trip to Fitchburg. But that trip seemed less likely every year that passed; and now, surveying the sudden harmony of this room, she lets it go entirely.

She even has Tom set up the tree, and hangs the birds and apples on it. It's four thirty when they finish, and she invites Tom out to supper for his labors. They go the Greeks on Moody Street; and she orders breakfast: eggs and sausage, home fries, and whole wheat toast with orange marmalade. Her favorite meal. The Greeks in back are having a loud argument as they enter. One of them comes out to take the order, then goes back to resume in stifled voices. The place is a hangout for her crowd; and John the Indian in the booth behind them winks. They've been coming here so long the Greeks feel comfortable carrying on their endless quarrels right in front of them. They speak in Greek, but the fight seems to be about the speediness or lack of it of the poor young man at the griddle.

I don't see how he can go any faster, says Henrietta, watching him toss her eggs and home fries into the bacon grease of the previous order without missing a beat.

I keep thinking about my party, she tells Tom. I'm going to win my grandson back, and I want him to meet you. He has a problem with drugs. I just want him to see your face and maybe someday you'll tell him your story.

Tom grins. Sure.

Her eggs come, and the good coffee. Tom has the raviolis. She thinks about her table, waiting to be laid with the good dishes she's had with her but never once used since she's lived here. And the little sapling with the tin birds and the little golden papier mache apples she hasn't used since Troy. Tonight she will light the lamps instead of the fluorescent tubes overhead.

Tom finishes his raviolis and wolfs the rolls. This is great, he says. Like a date, only you don't pay.

I'll be your girlfriend, Henrietta teases, and I won't present you with any more children, and ask for alimony…

Yeah!

Shall we have dessert?

You want dessert with breakfast?

Oh, I always have dessert with breakfast. My daughter Kate, when she was three or four, insisted on it.

Kate. Something about Kate...

Oh, then by all means, desert, he laughs.

We want hot fudge sundaes with the nuts, Henrietta tells the young man who's come out from behind the griddle and looks as if he's going to cry. Yes, I'll be your girlfriend, Henrietta teases..

What about Kate? It escapes her.

Yeah, that's what I need, he sighs. A woman won't give me kids. You got more furniture you need to hump?

Well, there are some little things I miss. I should have looked around while I was there. I only just today got interested in the livingroom, seeing how good it looked with the dining table...

We could go again.

Well, when you haven't anything else...

The only thing I need a man for anymore, she goes on, is to hump the furniture as you express it.

Your humping boyfriend.

Well listen. Nevermind that. Tell again; how long you're sober?

One month, one day and... He looks at the clock that's over the counter where the rapid argument in Greek continues like static. And five hours fifteen minutes.

I like to see your face when you say that. I have a grandson, you will meet him as I told you. He thinks peyote is the way to ecstasy. I'd like for him to see your face. Yes!

Before she goes to bed, she risks her neck climbing on a chair and getting down the good dishes. They were Lutie's second best set, Wedgewood. Plain white with fluted edges. Mountie had the best set, the flowered Spode, which Henrietta had never liked. Carol was to have had this second best set, the one they ate from when Lutie was having one of her rests.

One night. On the train somewhere west of Chicago. She had finally managed to sleep in her seat. And dreamed. The dream, when she thought of it later, had no elements of the macabre. She'd been in a department store, the kind where the elevator bell sounded every few seconds, and instead of a bell a loud horn had sounded and an empty elevator had opened before her and she'd entered it laden with packages, but found once she was in she had nothing in her hands. I'm dead, she'd thought. This empty elevator and the removal of the packages means I must be dead, or going to die. She woke to a fluttering heart. She'd had flutters in her heart all the previous day. She sat as quietly in her seat as she could until the dawn came to a cindery little town outside where huge snowdrifts were melting into puddles and some old pickups were coughing their way to life. And she thought about her oncoming death, what possessions she would leave and to whom.

Carol, who claimed she never slept, had been to the bathroom by then and was trying to do her stretches in the aisle. When she finished, Henrietta told her she was to have the Wedgewood and the Panama mahogany dining set if she were to die. Why? Carol asked; and Henrietta told her about the dream.

Who got in the elevator? Carol asked.

I did.

Jung says one person is often substituted for another in dreams, Carol said. It may not have been you.

Henrietta hadn't inquired who then it might have been.

XVIII

It's Lorraine M.'s anniversary at the big Saturday evening meeting at the Italian Church. Henrietta used to see her back when the group met at the hospital in the smaller doctors' lounge. Lorraine remembers Henrietta, but unfortunately Henrietta's forgotten her. The evening is a roast and everyone good humored, all the women wishing they had stories as funny as Lorraine, a whiskey voice as deep, could totter around like her on delicate ankles and high heeled pumps…

Like Henrietta she has a lot of stories. Twice she was in jail:

I didn't like jail, I tell you. Once I got so angry I flushed my blankets down the john and flooded the place, ha, ha!

Listen, she looks quizzically around the room. Didn't there used to be a lot of sofas in here. With the stuffing hanging out?

Yes, thinks Henrietta. The walls were lined with old sofas once. And we lolled about like Roman consuls at a banquet. Another feat of memory, she thinks. Like identifying Lucy by the little chairs. We sit on whatever is provided, she thinks. Still she doesn't remember this Lorraine.

But Henrietta recognizes in her the clown she is herself. Get old Yahweh splitting his sides up there in his heaven and all's forgiven was their rationale. You had to keep the earnest, Jesus people at bay; for all the program was pure rebirth and washing in the blood, you couldn't put it that way, though some did, discreetly.

Will the laughter last her? Henrietta wonders. Oh, she hopes so.

After the meeting, she goes with Tom and Lorraine to the Greeks, where she must pretend to remember Lorraine, and ends up convincing both of them she does.

There were sofas, she tells Tom. And all the stuffing was coming out the bottom. I wonder where they are now…?

I thought there were, says Lorraine. Everything runs all together after awhile. Even my first meetings in Florida seem like ancient history. I remember the night in jail more clearly. Ain't it awful, as my Eddie used to say.

Henrietta nods sympathetically. Yes, dear old Eddie, dear old sofas…

An argument in Greek has begun, between the little man at the griddle and the big man out front. I wonder why the big one doesn't simply fire him, Henrietta says.

He can't, says Tom. They're all family.

Do you think it's about sex? Henrietta, wonders. Or money?

What's the big fight about? Lorraine asks when the big man in the dirty apron comes to take their order.

The menu, he mutters, looking as if he could take a knife to someone any minute.

Well, that's nice to know, Henrietta says. We never would have asked. We were too scared.

Oh, nothing scares me, says Lorraine.

Henrietta orders breakfast with lots of whole wheat toast and orange marmalade. I hope they don't go and change the menu.

There are lots of other restaurants we could go to on Moody Street, says Tom.

No, it wouldn't be the same, says Henrietta. They often don't have orange marmalade. She doesn't want anything in her life to change; she could go on forever, she thinks, with life just about like it is now.

Megan's back at the Sunshine Club in a geriatric chair. The hospital can do no more. And, yes, it is the Virgin agitating her, although she sleeps a lot, and what she says is low, less urgent now, as if she's reached conciliation of some kind.

What the terms of this might be interests Henrietta, and she tries to have some kind of dialogue which includes, a little, the old Megan.

It's so surprising when I thought you hated the Church, its stand on contraception anyway... she says once after clearly hearing Megan say a bit of the Hail Mary, all the time agitating a rosary someone has put into her lap.

I beg your pardon? Megan murmurs.

It isn't any use. She asks if Megan would be interested in having something read, and tries to read her one of Flannery O'Connor's short stories, but Megan falls asleep. Even the book on Mozart cannot rouse her.

This mild woman isn't Megan of course. The only thing she might be grateful for is she isn't quite a caricature of herself, like Winnie and Adie—surely Adie's shouting about not letting the furnace go out, and Winnie's talk about how they used to wear pillbox hats, and bring boys home to meet their Pa, had some relation to their former selves—but this new Megan had no relation to the blasphemer that Henrietta knew. The black and bitter eyes seem to be turned around in her head and to look inward at something Henrietta can only guess at, but which has a certain dignity.

They wheel her without protest now to Reality Orientation. Once the date and weather and the next holiday are laid out to Bertha and Bobby Rosier's satisfaction, Henrietta reads her clips from newspapers about the progress of a Martian mission, and they fail to rouse the slightest interest from Megan. Whatever she is preoccupied with, it refuses any prompting from Reality.

It's hard for Henrietta to let it go. Perhaps it's temporary, like her heart

flutters which went away almost, once she'd been sober five years. She whispers
    Mozart
into Megan's ear every now and then, and looks for a spark. Or
    Schubert
But there's no reaction. Still, she keeps it up, though increasingly
discouraged.

I'll have to like it by myself, she tells herself one day when she is sitting near
to Megan playing a Scarlatti adaptation on her harp. It reminds her of when she
was a child and went another way from Mounty when he left off the alchemy
for physics and she turned to her construction of mud houses for turtles. I'll
just have to like it for myself, she told herself then.

  So she remonstrates with herself for needing the old Megan, and tries to take
an interest in Virgins—difficult for someone brought up in the Congregational
Church. The only thing she'd ever learned about The Virgin was from reading
Henry Adams. She was the "Mistress of the Seven Liberal Arts," she thought
she remembered, or some such thing. So, if that was true, why would she erase
from Megan's brain, a love of science, and music...?

Of course Megan's is the Irish Catholic's Virgin, far removed from anything
Henry Adams would have to say. Henry Adams was talking about Chartres
Cathedral and the simple workmen and townspeople who dedicated that great
work to Mary, as if it had been her dollhouse. Megan never could have read it;
in her right mind she would have shunned its topic; but it might have softened
her if she had...

Oh, I am absurd. It is some Irish Virgin she's conversing with, A Virgin I
could never fathom.

There was a Virgin sighted once, on the mountain that loomed over their
neighborhood in Maracay. All the servants and their mistresses were standing
out on their front gardens with binoculars trying to confirm the rumor. She
was among them, and had rummaged for Lutie's opera glasses in a trunk. But
it was impossible to be sure. One minute the apparition—there was definitely
something—would seem a piece of cloth, a flag or something, and the next, a
woman dressed in blue who genuflected, turned and walked away. With glasses,
it was no clearer than without; but only larger, she recalls. She had several looks
herself, and one moment was sure it was a figure in blue and the next not so
sure.

Next they said a priest was going up that barren mountain, where neither
flag nor Virgin plausibly could be, to investigate. But, like the opera glasses,
this investigation came to nothing as far as she ever heard: it seemed the Virgin
wasn't there when they got up there, reappeared when they returned. Then

disappeared for good some five days later. She was sure it was a very Latin kind of Virgin, one that would never visit one with horrors like this Irish one.

Oh, Henrietta, what do you know! I'll have to like this by myself, she mutters again, as she puts away her harp, then goes to help to open cans of green beans for lunch—well she wouldn't call them green, the green was boiled out of them some months or years ago. At least there isn't anybody here she worries about, except for Megan. They have no aspirations beyond, in Bobby's case, Santa's visit. And the things that interest them are, like these green beans, infinitely repeatable, like Isa's story of the brooch she fixed with pinesap on her way to the wedding, like these days which go around the calendar and begin again, and even Megan, now, is cured of her dissatisfactions. Perhaps it is God's mercy. She, Henrietta Rose, is not ready for it quite, but maybe Megan is.

The girl, Priscilla, who now attends the three of them at the lunch table, spooning pap, is the only one she can talk sense to. Rebecca is in her right mind of course, but her theories and her optimism have rendered her a bit of an imbecile.

Friday Owen

She calls Sheila. Tell me something Owen likes to eat. I want to make something new.

Well, he likes it when I make Chinese or Mexican.

Mexican. That's it.

At the Stigmatine's they're locked out and the group is outside stamping their feet in the cold. The coffeemaker's supposed to have the key, but someone says that he's "gone out". The trouble with giving keys to novices to open up and make the coffee—thus gaining a novice's necessary humility—is that they're the ones most likely to relapse like this.

At last, one of the brothers is waylaid and pulls a key ring from his habit. They put a small pot of water on for instant. Henrietta takes her boots off, rubs her feet.

It's a step meeting and they've reached the twelfth.

Why are here twelve? she wonders. Why not ten, fifteen? And were they led, those founders, every step of the way? No, they couldn't have been; there was a lot foolishness in the beginning, like the diet of stewed tomatoes, sauerkraut and Karo Syrup that Dr. Bob prescribed for drunks that came into his hospital. And taking drunks to an upstairs bedroom and making them get down on their knees and confess defeat.

The reading goes round the room. They will finish these fourteen pages and, next week start over with step one. She had a friend, once, an intellectual lady, couldn't abide it: You finish and start over again?

She understands this; as a reader, Henrietta liked to turn the pages, reach the end and start another book. This woman, however, ended up in a nursing home, receiving, smugly, her ration of booze, prescribed by doctor, brought to her each evening. Henrietta visited her just once. A terrible compromise, she sees it, like that lady poet took the Antabuse. She is glad that she, Henrietta Rose, had the sense to be simple for once. It could very well have escaped her. Still it was maddening sometimes, this circularity. Most of them could recite the whole step book by heart.

Her turn to read: she has the paragraph about...who wishes to be scrupulously honest, blah blah blah, unless it is the only way of staying sober, blah blah blah...?

Yet we are always honest with each other, she thinks. It never would occur to us to lie about our sober time. She's sure she wouldn't; no one would, and if the errant coffee maker that made us stand out in the cold comes back, he'll tell us exactly what he drank, how much, how sick he was... And if he comes back next week, we'll be back on the first step then, so he'll be able to start over, and the rest of us, to remember.

In spite of always failing the Memory Test, she thinks her memory is getting better. And her legs, it's certain, are improving. She often goes with one cane now, and in the house with none. But how can this old body be getting better, when a young and full of promise body, Carol's, couldn't?

There was a period, whose passing was unperceived by either of them, when she and Carol might have gathered up their luggage, settled with their landlord, Sr. Lomapelada, and gotten back over the border to the airport and flown back home to the East, or back to Oakland, to the Jungian circles and the dancers, or even to Seattle to the doctors: all places where they could have been less alone.

It wasn't to be. And Henrietta can recall a morning, helping Carol to the lounge chair in the shade of the veranera vine, and thinking: here, it is to be here. Up to that time, they'd only had a woman in to take their clothes and linens they had borrowed from the landlord out to wash them in the river. She came in Mondays to swab the floors and clean the kitchen. Miriam Herrera was her name; she'd migrated there from Guatemala. She had mentioned she had a daughter with some experience as a nanny; so Henrietta, on that same day, arranged to take her on to help with Carol. There was an extra bedroom, and this was given to the girl, who, like her mother, was a small barrel shaped woman tightly clad in black, who scurried about on fragile ankles. Her name was also Miriam; but this Miriam lived in and the other didn't. She was only twenty-two, though she looked older, and she had a little girl named Maria Luisa, five, whom she insinuated into the room a week or two after she'd come herself, at first for visits; and later, it seemed, permanently. Henrietta didn't mind; and Carol languidly watched the child play in the muddy gutters of the patio. It was the rainy season and a purple band of clouds assembled every morning at ten or so, and soaked the earth in early afternoon a couple hours; and then the sun came back.

It made a household of them to have the mother and the child. And Miriam, the mother, planned the dinner with Henrietta in the kitchen every morning, put the rice to cook, and ground the corn she'd cooked the night before and grilled tortillas to have with coffee for their breakfast; it was easy to pick up the local diet, drop their previous attempts at sandwiches and salads, meat and potatoes. Carol subsisted mainly on Miriam's soups, which ought to have been nourishing but weren't in her case; the weight dropped off her. Even height seemed to diminish.

She wasn't in pain, however, at this time of Miriam's first coming. Doctor Anzuátegui at the clinic, said she wouldn't be for a while. He ordered shots of vitamin B12, which a man from the pharmacy would come and give; and later, if it was necessary, he could give her morphine. A nurse could come as well, but Henrietta thought she'd try with Miriam for now. Carol didn't read, and hardly spoke. She took no part in these decisions Henrietta made. Of course she always asked Carol what she thought of this and that plan, but Carol always said it didn't matter; do whatever she thought best. She only roused herself a little to watch the child play, and even nodded when the child spoke. The fact that Carol had lost the language didn't matter to either of them. *Esta es mi casa*, the child said of a rectangle she'd drawn in mud, Y aquí el nene setting a little twig in center of her house, *Y aquí la mamá*. Here another twig. And the papa is at the war, she said, setting the third twig at a distance together with a little army of twigs.

XVIV

Henrietta Rose is going to give a Christmas party.

She walks, supported by the cart she uses back and forth to the IGA at Wallex Center, exchanges it for a store cart she wheels through produce, picking up cilantro she will need, long onions, and the oranges for the marinade. She won't select just any of the fresh hams they've set out, but will consult with the butcher. It's why she came this early, so he won't be taken up with others.

I want to order a fresh ham with the bone removed, she tells the butcher, who's been staring at her, because she's been talking to herself.

He brings out one that she rejects as being too large and fatty. The second is better. It's for a special occasion, she tells him. She hasn't had a consultation with a butcher since those days in Maracay when she used to go to the Frigorífico Lugo where the butcher flirted with her trying out his English and ignoring the urchins who came in for penny candy, making him open the packets and sell him just one, and the old men who could only buy one cigarette out of a pack, and the tight lipped local women who sniffed his chickens under the wing and insulted them, trying to get him to lower his price.

I should sniff under her arm, how she would like it! he expostulated to her once: *Mujer de mierda!*

The lovely leg is trimmed and netted. She takes it home and sets it to soak in orange juice, sprinkling over it chopped up garlic, scallions, and cilantro.

Oh, she's tired. All these memories tire her. She sits, then, at the half moon table, she's dragged home from Natick storage, uses in the kitchen now, to eat her solitary meals. It's very small, but Geoffrey manages, after threading himself carefully around the yellow plastic sugar bowl, the eggshell porcelain creamer from West Boylston, and a set of pretty pewter candlesticks, to seat himself just behind her teacup and regard her rather coldly, in spite of all the trouble he has taken to be near her. I haven't any creamers for you, she tells him. She brings him creamers from the Greeks where she and Tom go nearly every day for coffee now. He blinks, resumes his stare.

She howled and ranted, once, in the presence of a cat, the same—she thinks it was—striped yellow tom that was run over on route 62, the one that Carol buried. What must it think of me? She'd wondered at the time. As soon as the children left for school, this...performance of hers commenced: the howls, the moans, she couldn't help herself. And only the cat to witness with his yellow stare.

The dog...where was the dog, then? She was a lovely dog and her soulful, beagle eyes would have expressed compassion... No, it was before they had the dog; it must have been.

Before they all came home, she got control, made supper, lay next to Gerald in the bed until he fell asleep; then getting up and, stifling her whimpers, shutting herself away in the furthest reach of the house, Gerald's study, drinking and pacing about till morning; sometimes she fell unconscious on the leather couch in there, and Carol came to wake her before eight, to sit at the breakfast table for appearance's sake.

One of these mornings Carol didn't find her. She had taken the car and driven herself to a fashionable madhouse.

Was that alcoholism? Carol later asked—it was while they were on one of the train trips—referring to that morning. We thought you'd gone bonkers...

Yes, it was, she'd said. I hadn't any business in a madhouse.

And was it awful there?

You can't imagine! A snakepit for all its beautiful look outside. I'd hardly been in there ten minutes and I'd called your father to get me out...He wouldn't. I can't blame him now. It was Lutie finally signed me out. Your Grandmother.

But then, said Carol, puzzled, you went into... other ones.

Well, yes, I found the good ones, public ones. I told my lovely stories in three or four of them. I hadn't any business there, in any of them; but I loved them. Unlike the first one, where they'd have kept me till I rotted, these others always treated you nicely, turned you out within some reasonable time...

She wonders whether Gerald really would have left her in that first place, where she'd known right off that all the others there were wives and children of the fed up wealthy, who would never see outside again. He must have been fed up. Poor man. He'd always had, before, a staff of servants to fill in for her deficiencies.

And was it possible, had they stayed in foreign parts, she might have been maintained on booze, and in society, until she died, like Lutie, like that woman poet...at a fairly advanced age? How horrible.

But they had come back here. Gerald always thought of research as his place; and research wasn't done in India, in South America, in those days. It was more like cooking, what he did there, he said. But he never did get back to research. It was cooking that he did in New York State, in spite of changing companies a couple times, and losing all his pensions, it was cooking.

He should have, like his parents, stayed in or near the universities. He should have gone to war, come back and finished a PhD. He might have if he hadn't had a premonition that she'd fail him, give him flock of children and then fail him.

She'd even run away to Lutie, once. A widow, then, Lutie lived in an apartment in the Vendome Hotel in Boston, with a nurse, who portioned out the pills and booze. She had an extra room if the nurse lived out. They tried it for a couple months. The children were in college, then, except for Charles, who'd dropped out.

So Gerald and Charles lived like two bachelors, cooked for themselves; in Gerald's case it seemed to do him good; he looked sleeker, gained some weight; talked more. And Henrietta learned she couldn't live with Lutie. Lutie discussed and fretted over every minor decision—her life so girded about with money, bankers, lawyers, no decision left to Lutie could be major. But Henrietta must accompany her to the bank to speak to one of its vice presidents, merely to cash a check, or to make the small deposits from her funds. Lutie liked to keep some of it in her own hands in order to make as many complications as she could for her custodians.

They woke from their drugged sleep at nine or ten; and Lutie, suffering— she now knows—from incipient, unacknowledged Korsakofian loss of short term memory, would ask her if she'd slept well. A polite question. Lutie always was polite. And Henrietta would answer, trying not to be sullen; she wasn't fourteen any more, an age when her moodiness was a family joke. And Lutie'd then report on her own sleep, which she looked on as fretfully as she did her banking transactions. Then as they sat down to coffee and toast and scrambled eggs which Henrietta fixed each morning, Lutie would inquire again, if she had slept well; and she would have to answer a second time. Would there be a third? she'd wonder with increasing irritation, till it came, invariably, in Lutie's ingratiating, fretful tones, I suppose you slept well? And Henrietta, answering as patiently as possible, Oh, yes, fine, thought she'd scream.

Of course she'd slept. She'd take her minor tranquilizers with a glass of sherry, at their dinner, sent up from the dining room, or occasionally, when Lutie was up to it, taken in the Vendome Room; another glass at eight or so, to keep her mother company until the nurse appeared with the ration from the bottle she alone had access to, and Lutie's other medication. They were zonked by nine.

She went back to Gerald at the end. He was sick, and they needed each other. After he died, she lived and drank alone, a year or two, in a lovely old brownstone townhouse in Troy.

One time Gerald's old father visited. He had outlived Gerald by fifteen years. The old man had gone to college there and wanted to see old colleagues, as well as Henrietta, whom he always favored. It was while he was there, the embarrassment of walking into his room, the guestroom, happened.

They'd both gone to bed about ten; and Henrietta, who hadn't had her ration of vodka yet, because of this visit, took the bottle into the bed with her and finished it. At about three am, she'd gotten up to go to the bathroom, and then, all unaware of what she was doing, had gone into the guest bedroom and lain down in the bed with Gerald's father.

He hadn't even waked. She slept beside him till dawn, then woke and tried to ascertain where she was, finally recognizing with horror it was her own guest room. She tells this story to great hilarity in certain meetings. As far as she knows, no one else has ever gotten away with anything similar.

That day, she called for help, and went, by bicycle, to her first meeting. It was in a room of a grand old Presbyterian church that overlooked the city, and she remembers that it had been endowed by one of the early owners of an ironworks. She doesn't, however, remember a thing that was said in these early meetings. It was the bicycle riding she's convinced, that won those first three months from alcohol. But the pills continued. She called up AA Central Service, inquiring about the policy on pills...Throw them out, the person said.

But I won't sleep.

Well run around the block a couple times; you'll sleep.

But I'm exercising already, riding a bicycle...

Throw them out, is all the wretched woman would say.

She didn't. She bought a bottle of vodka; so much for them. She thought they might have tried, at least, to be a little understanding.

She was still thinking about what it had cost her, getting these pills in the first place, once they'd come back to this country and you couldn't just walk in pharmacies and ask for whatever! Here, you had to present yourself with symptoms, to a doctor.

She'd drink first, before she saw Dr Milstein, so that she could free associate: Lutie's upturned pumps, the bottom of a stair, foreshortened body of her mother. And a corridor that disappeared, and reappeared...

And this corridor, you imagine it often now?

Oh, all the time, she'd told him. It's why I am afraid to sleep. A dreadful lie.

Her case was fascinating to Dr. Milstein, and to Dr. Benda, who came next. They seemed eager to help her and never picked up her drinking. She never could have held them in her spell without the vodka. She was a poet on the vodka. She was a case. She imagined Dr. Benda so eager that she suspected him of following her about on streets, peering in her windows, and wanting to ravish her. There were several versions of the fantasy: in one, he took her against her will; and others, she was willing. She walked around all day, enveloped in these dreams.

No, the booze wasn't easy to give up. Then, one day, she came out of a blackout with bicycle grease all over her leg as evidence that she'd gone out after finishing a quart of vodka, lost her pocketbook with her wallet, credit cards, and left the front door wide open. She threw the bottles out.

I'm Henrietta, I'm an alcoholic. I remember when I said those words aloud the first time.

Henrietta is speaking in the Club Surrender. Tom's two month anniversary.

It was the evening after I'd spent the day on the telephone cancelling my credit cards, after waking from a blackout and finding that I'd lost my wallet.

I had been going to meetings, big speaker meetings till then. I'd never had to say those words before, until this evening for a change I went to a group that met a couple blocks away from where I lived. I'd never gone there, didn't want my neighbors knowing... Well, it was a beginner's group and they sat around a table, introducing everybody. When it came my turn, I had to say it:

I'm Henrietta, I'm an alcoholic.

It was like I'm walking blind into your arms, leaving my old way behind, and joining...you. I had a lot of admiration for you by that time; I'd been around a year ignoring all the rules. I still ignore a lot of rules; but never did walk back across a kind of line I crossed that night.

When Henrietta finally gave up the pills as well as booze, the issue of course was sleep. I won't sleep, she told herself, I'll never sleep again.

She said it violently, like saying, Frig you, Lutie. You and your everlasting sleep! I simply won't. It was a purifying anger. I simply won't sleep!

I'll...do something else instead! I will! But what? I'll weave. I'll buy a weaving loom. I'll sew a quilt, like Nummie, Lutie's mother, did—her southern grandmother, who sewed on with tiny stitches her little houses, trees, and children cut from scraps. I'll read Cervantes and Saint Teresa in the original... I'll learn to read in French.

It was the Saint Teresa of Ávila, and the French that did it. She didn't sleep a moment, she could swear it, for three weeks; and then, every night with few exceptions, she fell asleep with a volume in Spanish or in French, kicked to one side in bed, having read a single page... and slept till morning.

The biggest miracle of any of what followed.

XX

In bed, she finishes a story by Herman Melville in an old college text book she found in the Natick storage. It's all defaced by her callow freshman observations in purple ink and an immature hand she forgets she ever had: Purity, Influence of Emerson? Evil, Innocence. blah, blah, blah.

She had loved these books. Lutie never knew the gift she'd given her, sending her to college, even if it was just to get a suitable father for her children. Callow as she'd been, when she scrawled in these margins in purple ink, she thinks sometimes she might have been a serious person.

And here's her old copy of Mrs. Dalloway.

Clarissa Dalloway, oh yes! She used to recognize something of herself in Clarissa Dalloway.

Clarissa Dalloway is on the brink of her party, as Henrietta Rose is on the eve of hers.

Tuesday paint

Like AA, Warren never cancels for any reason, not even Christmas Eve. She's grateful to him. This closing down of everything because of holidays is awful to a person living alone. You can't buy a stamp, or cash a check, or go to the library. Of course the van won't come so she has to take the city bus, if they're still running. Oh of course they are, on reduced schedule. She'll have to leave a good amount of time for getting there.

She's eager to finish a new painting, of the house in West Boylston; this one with Lutie in the livingroom smoking, legs crossed gracefully, hair piled up the way she sometimes wore it. It's another of her paintings with walls torn away, so you can see the rooms; and, in the kitchen, she'd begun a figure of a woman working at a sink, and Henrietta wasn't sure last Thursday if it's Hulda Engbretsen or Nummie. But she realizes now, of course, it was Miz Lili, as they were supposed to call her, or Nummie as they actually called her.

Lately, she likes to think of Nummie. Nummie loved the kitchen. For all her gentle upbringing, she spent more time in the kitchen and in the sewing room than in drawing rooms. Where Lutie had been a fretful housekeeper, wanting everything nice as the next person, still resenting the bother, or fearful of the results, Nummie used to relish stationing herself in the kitchen, directing the cooks and maids, jumping, herself, to chop things finer than they could, to taste and season, whomp the bread dough with an energy exceeding any cook she ever had.

Oh, Lutie could sometimes carry off something of Nummie's kitchen flair, but it lacked her joy, she sees; Nummie did it out of joy. She could have changed her station anytime with Hulda Engbretsen, with her own cook at home in Louisville, and still been happy.

The same with handwork, yes, she can remember Nummie setting out a quilt, the little houses, cut out freehand, trees with birds in them, and children jumping rope and playing hopscotch, cut from scraps of printed cloth and sewed with tiny, patient stitches, joyous work.

Like mine. She fastens on her boots and takes a deep, slow breath. I might have learned it anytime from her...But then I might have died like Lutie, never learning... She walks to the corner, avoids ice patches; it won't do to fall today, before her dinner.

The Chinese boy, who lives next door, waves and wavers on his bicycle down the center of the lane. You ought to wear a helmet, Henrietta calls.

Oh, yes, he grins, and stops to greet her. He was in some student demonstration, the Fahey woman told her, and had to escape the country with some help from Brandeis University. Now he's cleaning houses till he starts his studies.

Seriously, she says slowly and distinctly. I was hit once when I used to ride.

It was in Troy. She ran into another woman on a bicycle and flew into a bush. And Priscilla. Priscilla was knocked down on Moody Street that time.

Oh, yees, he grins politely, hasn't an idea what she's saying.

And you ought to have a light. I see you go at night.

Yess, yess. He makes a little bow.

She gives up. Listen. She fumbles in her purse and finds the notebook and the pen she keeps, and writes, Come tomorrow. To dinner. Three pm.

He reads and understands: Yes, oh yes. Thenk you. Thenk you.

She sees her bus coming and waves frantically; he's about to pass her.

What's your name?

Chang.

Chang. She writes it down in her notebook as soon as she's settled in her seat. She will buy Chang a helmet for Christmas. Another guest, but with the leaf and extra chairs she actually can seat two people more. She plans to shop at Wallex Plaza on her way home. She has a gift for Jason, and a nice saucepan for the cohabiting couple, but has forgotten something for the fat child.

Well, says Warren when she walks in late. We thought that you're like all the other ladies, doing what-they-call-it, last minute shopping.

Well, I plan to, but mine is very rapid. She fumbles with the tubes in such a hurry, now she knows who the kitchen figure is, her darling Nummie. She has to calm herself and take deep breaths.

It's only Mike and Warren today; the troll painter and the other watercolor ladies absent, shopping lengthily she guesses. Mike and Warren are discussing World War II as usual. Not a sign of holiday decoration, it reminds her of that night she spent in an Alcathon, her first year sober, that derelict hall, her sleeplessness, her giddiness, her thankfulness for no sign of a holiday. She couldn't have borne it. Only now can she bear a holiday. What time she wasted, what precious time...

The figure in the armchair, Lutie, is just right, the airy posture, the absent stare of the large eyes. She makes the kitchen figure, more substantial, bigger than the refrigerator, she's standing next to...that's all right. She remembers a weaving from Ecuador she had once where a man towers over the house he stands next to. And Nummie had a big frame. You saw it when she lost the weight at start of that long illness, when her breasts, released from corsets, sagged past her middle. She will paint her in her time of health, she decides.

You really want her that big? says Mike behind her.

Oh, yes, she was big, important...

Who's that guy up in the attic? Warren wants to know.

Oh, my brother Mounty. She'll get to him next.

After the alchemical messes and the investigation of falling bodies that followed, Henrietta turned to her mud houses and her dreams of horses; and Mounty turned to contests in the newspapers and magazines. It brought them back together briefly, for she had to participate of course; it increased the odds. In fact, Mounty even invented a third sibling, who entered the contests as Benno Montague. Henrietta was valuable as she was as clever as Mounty at writing jingles and answering riddles and finding hidden cats and owls and bunnies in forest scenes.

They never won; it flummoxed Mounty. Must be the mail, the kids live closer, judges get their answers first. He spent his money on special delivery sometimes, and nothing. Just a matter of keeping up. Statistically we have to win sometime. The odds...

And that was where he ended up. A statistician. He studied the subject, that is, in college. Then he worked for firms that played the market, bonds she thinks it was.

She doesn't know what happened after that. She lost him somewhere, up there in the attic, during the puzzles sometime. She never shared his anxiety to win the way she shared the messes with him and the leaping out of trees. What did they need money, prizes, for? They had as many bicycles and electric toys as any child could want. What would they have done with money anyhow? She will have to leave him for now as a smudgy figure up there in the dark. She cannot think where Mounty might have saved himself...where she...How careless she had been, and stupid.

Mounty won a scholarship to the London School of Economics, and married there, another student: Lovely girl from Cornwall. A redhead; and they'd had a pretty daughter with a head full of copper ringlets.

Beautiful children. Her own young family: how beautiful they'd been; all of them, not just Carol. There, she might have stuck. Had they been undone, she and Mounty, by Lutie's evanescences? They might equally have been held fast by Nummie's strong presence in the kitchen...

She must ask him. She must see him. She'd consulted enough doctors over the years with these questions. Why had she never thought to ask her brother? Instead of bothering him about his drinking, which got them nowhere, she might have inquired with him where this closing in process, this letting go of spouses and children, had begun with each of them.

As she finishes painting the row of envelopes addressed to contests, she wonders how could they have been so intent, so organized, as children; and so careless as adults.

There is none of the usual blather today. Mike patiently paints each quill of his pheasant's breast, knowing his precision will repay and people will marvel at the realism...Warren squints at his latest landscape, brushes in a veil of distance over some small hills in the background. Possibly he'll sell it; more likely not. A capable painting, any case. He'd been a capable engineer at one time...capable father, husband. Now he is a capable painter. Such quirks of fate as produced a painter like Henrietta Rose had not occurred to him; yet he can admire her struggles and her occasional victories, as in this arc of envelopes sailing out of a house whose front has been removed to expose its rooms...

There is a rummage sale upstairs in the church hall. She finds a used helmet and also a bike light, and a perfectly new set of colored pencils for Sheila's child. All for three dollars. Goes home in high spirits with the money she's saved.

If only Mounty will come. Mounty must come. She gets home at four o'clock and spoons the marinade over her leg of pork, then calls him to renew her invitation. He hasn't committed. He doesn't get out much, his arthritis bothers...

You must, Henrietta begs; it's my first dinner party in...sixteen years, she figures hastily. It's important to me.

He'll try. He'll see. She isn't hopeful.

I think so much lately, about you as a boy, she says. Do you remember the experiments, the contests?

Oh, my god, he drawls.

Mounty, come... she says, attempting to bridge all the years, all the failures. She hears him clear his throat.

I'll try, he says.

Come early, she says, knowing how his afternoons are. Come as soon as you get up. The earliest train. Call when you get here, and I'll have someone pick you up.

Charles calls her at ten. She's already in bed with Clarissa Dalloway. He will come. If he doesn't show up it's because his car has broken down.

If they all come, she will have enough chairs but not enough room at the table. She will have to serve buffet. That will be all right. Buffet changes the character of a party, she well knows. It might be an advantage for this particular event; she will be able to circulate and enliven any dull sub-groups. It is a strategic advantage to a hostess not to be held in a fixed position at a table, where one is helpless to rescue any guests sunk in dullness at the far end of the table. The Enemy of Dullness, that is Henrietta Rose!

Clarissa Dalloway on the brink of her party. How true it is, the confusion, the forebodings, as Mrs. Dalloway's party begins. Always Henrietta had these sinking moments, largely because she invited people who interested her, Henrietta, and would not necessarily interest each other.

And then, someone in Clarissa's rooms distractedly bats a curtain blowing in at a window; and this is a signal her party is a success. Of course: The glowing silver, the silk upholstery, has become a mere background, at that moment, to the talk. The curtain is something one can push around to get comfortable. Oh, it's thrilling to read. How could she know? Such truth!

Clarissa wants of Peter Walsh something similar to what Henrietta wants from Mounty. Does she find it as the party progresses? No, it seems not. She has no time. "Later, Later," she must tell old friends. And the two unconventional ones, Peter and Sally, meet up and seem to agree that Clarissa is vain and superficial, a dry social stick, while they are still alive and open to adventure. Sally invites Peter, who is a failure, who is in love, to meet her merchant husband in her provincial estate. Clarissa's husband isn't in the cabinet, as everyone expected. He is a stick, they conclude. And Clarissa's daughter loves her father best; her mother embarrasses her: Here is my Elizabeth, she says affectedly to

Peter.

But, but...We know how Clarissa once felt about Sally Seton. We know Richard's wordless love for his wife, his expressed love for his daughter, his simplicity for which Clarissa broke off her friendship with Sally. And we know Clarissa's joy as she breaks into her fifty-second year, gathering them all together, standing them upright in the vase like so many roses she will paint. Ah, no, she is no stick. And she is selfless. Peter's meaning will not be revealed to her: Later, later... It is Peter who sees. Yes, here she is...filling him with terror and ecstasy.

Henrietta Rose hardly sleeps; Tom will come at ten, she thinks; he will pick up Mounty. Charles could come any time. What will these people find to say to each other? How will she explain Tom to Jason? to Charles? They must talk to each other at least enough to allow her to put things on the table, she frets.

Of course, it won't be till the last moment she can plan on Charles's—or Mounty's, or anybody's—appearance or non-appearance, so plans must be kept fluid and the table not set till the end. Or would it be best to simply plan buffet style, as if she'd chosen it from the first as the more festive alternative. The pork could then be done early and served cold...Yes, this is what she will do. The table will be lovely spread with all the dishes, rather than putting them out on kitchen counters.

Yes. She gets out of bed and writes it in her notebook:

Buffet Style.

And her wisdom is confirmed when, sometime after two, the phone rings, and she hears the wan voice from the bottom of a well:

It's Debbie.

Oh dear God! When phones ring in the early hours like this, her head is always filled with thoughts of gore and mayhem.

I'm downtown. I got the last train at twelve, and I'm in the station.

She has forgotten who this person is.

Can I come? I'll walk. I didn't drink. They all did, but I didn't.

The goats, she thinks. Something about goats.

I'll just come in and sleep on the couch...I didn't drink.

This last reassures Henrietta. I'll leave the door open and a blanket on the couch.

She gets up and pulls blanket and pillow out of the closet, unlocks the door, and falls asleep. In the morning, she's forgotten the conversation, is shocked to find the body on her couch; cries out and wakes the girl.

I called; you said to come. I walked from the station. I didn't drink... says

Debbie, sitting up.

'Twill be your theme in glory, sings Henrietta, thinking of the old hymn.

All the others were drinking. I went with them. I couldn't be alone. You said to come.

Oh, I'm sure I did. I didn't write it down. I was too sleepy, so I don't remember. We'll have some coffee. Today is my big day, I'm throwing a party... she grins.

Meat in Oven

says her agenda for the morning. She spoons the marinade over for last time and sticks it in. Then puts on the coffee.

The girl is fumbling in her backpack. That smells wonderful...I knew I should call...somebody in the...

Meetings.

Meetings, yes. He even gave me numbers, Tom, the person you intro...

But you did, you called me, and you didn't drink.

They laugh.

I was so crazy. A social worker came to see how I was doing with these children, THAT AREN'T MINE. And one of them kept crying and falling down; it never acts, like, that way usually, and got an egg on its head and I was feeling like a monster because I couldn't pick it up—the woman's standing in the way—and she picks it up acts like she's some kind of savior to these children I'm trying to take care of, who...

Aren't yours.

And yes, I started screaming that at her, and so she says they'll have to take them; there are too many dogs and goats; it isn't sanitary, so take the fucking goats! I screamed, I lost control; and later, when they took us down to file a complaint against us, I was rolling on the floor and kicking at some partition till my foot went through it, then, while they were phoning for police, I just ran out and down the street to The English Room, and out the back door with some old friends.

I did try to take care of those kids, she says more calmly.

I'm sure you did.

And now I've abandoned them.

Henrietta can't remember who these kids are, and how the girl came by them, but the goats sound familiar. She sets some coffee and toast on the table, sits down opposite her and looks into her face. A teary and disordered face, but sober, she can see.

None of it matters, she says. But that you're sober. I used to take a drink sometimes, so that, I told myself, I could remain a lady. That was the sheerest folly. You have to explore the depths of the unladylike—as you are doing right now—says Henrietta Rose in her present wisdom.

She hopes that Tom will put in an appearance soon. I'm having a party today, she tells the girl. It must be meant that you should come.

Oh but I shouldn't stay. You have your...

I have some people I'm trying foolishly to save. Some of them are related to me, and some others are some people I find much more interesting and hopeful, for example, a boy whose cerebellum I hope to preserve until he can go to Brandeis, and Tom, who needs a woman like me, who won't marry him, and you must promise not to marry him either.

Oh no! I wouldn't!

But Henrietta doesn't trust her. Oh, well, she can't control the world. Does Debbie know how to peel potatoes? Not really. Oh well, we'll have instant instead, it's ten already. She has to start her gelatin with fruit.

Then Mounty calls. He came!

Since Tom hasn't arrived yet, she must send Debbie back down on the Lexington bus to collect him. What is he wearing? she asks him.

An old blue chesterfield. Rimless glasses, not much hair, and medium height, she tells Debbie. Try to grab him and get right back on the bus. Just call out you're looking for a Mr. Mounty Pierce-Montague. She sends her off with a borrowed hat and scarf.

He's come! She barely can believe it. And before Debbie can return with Mounty, Charles comes and stands around the kitchen drinking coffee with Tom, who arrives right after, talking about the fuel line on his truck. She gets the fruit mold in the refrigerator and tries to collect herself.

Then Mounty comes; he's shy with Debbie, with the others; and he looks very old. She tries not to be shocked. His eyes seek hers; why must there be such confusion if it's I you want to see? is his appeal.

But later, later, she signals. See my life; this is my life, these people...

And the meat must come out; and coats taken to the bedroom, and the cranberry punch set out, and the celery and olives. And now Chang has come; his eyes also seek hers, but such is the nature of these mixes of hers, their unknown factors, that it turns out that Mounty in his solitude has taught himself Mandarin. Oh, he always could amaze her. And so he and Chang are soon deep in conversation on the little love seat she's brought from Natick and put in the alcove by the double window, Chang's pocket dictionary open between them.

Jason, then, comes in with Owen...has Sheila left him? No, she's picking her daughter up at her ex-husband's family, will be along; but both of them look dangerous and Debbie—who as recently as yesterday was kicking in partitions of a social service agency—applies herself to soothe. And Tom, is orbiting around Debbie, fixed as any asteroid, in spite of all he's ever learned. Whatever happens, they probably won't drink is all that Henrietta can predict.

But Jason must, and Mounty must; a discreet bottle of Hennessy's and some glasses stand behind her bowl of cranberry punch. Henrietta calmly casts her eye over it and all the rest.

The reconstituted potatoes are heated up again in butter, and the vegetable medley is tossed into a white sauce, and the fragrant pig is cooled down to a perfect temperature for slicing. She calls Tom to carve it. A pan of its juices bubbles on the stove; she pours it into Lutie's old gravy boat and carries it in to the table.

It's served, she calls, and pushes Chang and Mounty toward her table. It all looks fine to her. Nothing tastes, as usual; but she takes a plate to one of little tables Sheila's loaned her and feeds herself absently, wishing she could listen in on Mounty, but knowing she'd inhibit them in their bilingual groping. Owen, across the room, looks pale but handsome in a figured sweater, probably an early gift. He's stretching upward, as Carol did when she was twelve or so, the long bones, the fine lifted jaw. The Rose looks.

Come to me, she calls him, tall, pale flamelike figure, away from the heavy child with her dark curls who is sinking into the sofa, away from his teasing. The child will probably never become his stepsister. How dreadful it is, the children waiting around their entire precious childhoods while the adults in charge of them sort themselves out. Sheila is a nice person, but if she won't stick, Henrietta can't waste time on her.

Owen comes, and folds himself at her feet. You're growing so tall. And that sweater is very flattering, she tells him.

I hate it, he says. It isn't my taste.

What is your taste?

Black, he says. All my clothes black. And my hair long.

Like my friend Tom.

Owen studies Tom, who is standing in the kitchen doorway: I like his boots.

I used to find him rather shocking, she muses. Now I hardly notice his taste.

How come he's your friend?

He takes me to meetings in his truck. He's been taking me to get my furniture out of storage.

And that's his chick?

You mean Debbie? Well that just happened, I'm afraid. I invited them both. It might have been a mistake...

And how do you know her?

She calls me up when she's in trouble. She was in quite a jam yesterday, so she came here and slept.

And why does she call you? He's clearly intrigued.

I wonder that myself. I must think about it. I mean we're both drunks, but there are lots of other drunks she could have called besides me...

You mean you drink together?

No, no. We try together not to drink. It can be interesting. She's tempted to expand here, but decides not.

I hate Newton, he says. I wish I could live here.

Newton schools are very good. You might be grateful someday.

I went a whole semester without ever finding my homeroom. When they found out, they put me in a prison with the mental cases, and we do art all day. Anything I learn, I learn by myself in the library. Sheila thinks they should put me with the smart kids.

Sheila seems pretty sensible...I spend a lot of time with mental cases myself. It doesn't do any harm. But you should be getting an education.

Dad says I'm mental. Mom's whole family is mental.

He's probably just manipulating her, she thinks.

I don't want to talk about it, he says.

No, not a holiday subject. And yet she's glad he's circling around her, testing her; he'll maybe call her up out of his depths some night. Like Debbie.

She moves on to put out the cake Sheila brought, longing suddenly to talk to someone her own age, to Mounty, before he breaks into the Hennessey botttle, still unopened. He and Jason probably providing their own little bottles, of the variety that fit in jacket pockets.

She finds Mounty talking now to Charles, while Chang is looking at a book he's pulled from her bookcase. Jason is sitting all by himself in the alcove. Time for a little hostess intervention.

She takes her little gifts from under tree; she's slipped checks into cards for Tom and Debbie, so has something for everyone but Mounty. She really didn't believe he'd come, she realizes. But he'll understand, and he's consented to stay over on her couch, so she'll have him, if not tonight, tomorrow...

We'll spend billions to excavate it centuries later, I thought one day, when I was driving around to garage sales, Mounty is saying to Charles.

Yeah, Charles breaks in. Listen, once when I was cleaning out this house, this woman...A book, I thought, A coffee table book about garage sales...With mostly photographs. Someone ought to do it. I've thought of doing it myself!

Their precious junk, she thinks. Can such a thing as a love of junk be enclosed in a gene?

She starts to distribute the gifts. Sheila has brought some of the children's gifts, and a beautifully wrapped box for Henrietta, so there are a great many. And little by little they all fall into the ritual, sitting facing the sapling with the birds in it, and opening their surprises. She is most excited about her gift to Chang, watching him awkwardly take off the paper and examine the lamp, which is the kind that fits against the wheel and generates its own power.

He must put it on immediately, she tells him; and asks Tom if he will help. The bike is in the hallway just downstairs, so all the men troop down. She and Sheila clear some of the plates, and she hears her party settle into its rhythm of calm and excited voices, of younger ones banging in and out and looking for tools in drawers. She takes a cup of coffee then. Coffee always tastes. And a slice of the plum cobbler Sheila's brought. She can taste it too. Delicious. She has a second piece and says to Sheila, who's standing at the sink and running hot water over plates, that she wishes she could stay with Jason. For Owen's sake.

Oh, Henrietta...

Of course, if you're so terribly unhappy...He's not your child. It just seems you're more...flexible than his father. And Owen does seem to care for you.

Jason does care about him, Sheila says.

Of course. And I know his mother was just as awkward as Jason in trying to do something for him. And then her illness...

Oh, Henrietta!

Well, it was just the wrong time in his life, for them to give up on each other...And now you two giving up...

But he's not the only child this ever happened to, and I think he's playing on everyone's sympathy, and we shouldn't let him do that.

Yes, you're right. And the worst thing is that his mother went off a world away to die, and it must be this huge blank to him. I hope I can tell him about it sometime. Carol wanted me to. I think it's why she forgave me everything and went off with me to Mexico. At first we were looking for a miracle, but at the end, she wanted me to carry something back to her child.

Sheila puts a plate very gently into the sink. No matter what happens, I'll stay in touch. I promise.

You're a good girl. I hope you're happy.

Oh, happy, Sheila says. I think maybe happy is overrated.

I'm happy. Henrietta thinks. I'm happy tonight.

They go back into the living room. Mounty is lying on the couch which will be his bed later, and Charles is still talking very excitedly about old music boxes. She recalls her parties in Sogamoso, the musicians they hired to play merengues earlier in the evening for dancing, would become mellow after midnight, and often one of the members would step forward; and, while the others strummed softly, begin to recite a long story, in rhyme, about some taxi driver or bricklayer and his lover who is a black-eyed waitress with *ojeras*; and he dies when his taxi falls into a gorge, or a building collapses; and the black-eyed waitress dies in giving birth to a child with lips like roses and skin as white as the Child Jesus. Oh, it was sad; and no one could believe he could recite the whole thing by heart. But people did that there. Taxi drivers—who might be musicians at night—did drive around with volumes of poetry on the seat beside them, she had seen it.

But here is Chang to thank her for his gift. She lays a finger on his temple: Now you wear the helmet, she tells him; and he nods effusively. I know a girl who had an accident, and a helmet saved her brains...

He nods and smiles.

Mounty has been standing by listening to this. How old do you think Chang is? he asks her.

Oh maybe twenty-one...

He's thirty-four. He used to teach philosophy at a university, until they sent him to harvest potatoes.

Oh many potatoes, Chang puts in, and we must eat them too, without any salt or oil even. Only potatoes, for three years.

Oh, dear!

I cannot eat potato again, not ever, he says.

And I made potatoes... she begins, and feels inadequacy of her response. What can one say? And was that all you had to eat?

Oh yes, potatoes. All.

But he is smiling and his face is rosy, calm, except for the perturbation of finding words in English.

But you are happy. Happy here?

Oh, yes, happy.

They used to ask her that in Sogamoso, native women. *Estás contenta aquí?*

Ah, yes. What else was one to say with such a small vocabulary. Probably Mounty could pull a nuanced answer out of Chang. She'll have to limit herself to saving his skin from traffic along the Lexington Road.

When did you find the energy, the leisure, to learn Mandarin? she asks Mounty. Brains, I mean of course, Henrietta amends.

He settles back on her sofa; he looks quite at home there. Evenings, he says. I used to take a year and read, in a language I chose, every evening for an hour or so. Children's books and easy grammar to start; and, by the end of the year, I found I had this, reading knowledge. It's interesting, I find Chang did the same. His English is quite extensive; he's simply never heard it spoken till now. He taught German and Russian he tells me; and had never heard them spoken.

And did you hope you'd travel, use these languages?

Not necessarily. I was after reading knowledge.

Ah, Mounty, I don't know you...I don't know you... So many years...

Yes.

I think all the time about when we were children. What were we doing, stirring up all those messes, jumping out of trees...?

We were recapitulating the history of our race, of humankind, I'd say.

Whatever do you mean?

Well, the early belief in magic, then alchemy; and, finally, the dawn of reason, science...

She is thoughtful, watching him. He hasn't started drinking, and his hands, she notes, are tensely clasped behind his head.

And you think all children do the things we...?

We were allowed a certain latitude, we were gifted perhaps, in some small measure. He unclasps his hands to wave his right one above his head. It trembles slightly, and he wedges it back behind his head.

But I...I don't believe I ever believed in magic, she says. I hated fairy tales. I couldn't read Alice or any of those fanciful stories until I was in my twenties, when I read them all, as literature. I was some kind of thorough scientist, or thorough cynic, right from the start. I just thought if you mixed enough things together, something would happen... Remember when you started sending off to contests, and you told me about "odds"? You said we had to win if we could send enough?

Oh, lord, yes!

Well, I had a similar notion about the potions we mixed up: You put enough...substances together, something would ferment. Now was that irrational magic? Something did happen. All kinds of smells and colorful molds and bubbling did occur...

But it never turned to gold, he says.

I never thought it would! she cries, Did you?

Ah, yes, I did, he says. For all I can remember. I haven't thought of this in years. I wonder you remember...

It's all that's left to me intact, she says. I write my obligations down, I don't forget the faces of old friends; but, beyond that, what I did yesterday, what I did half a minute ago, is like a slate, wiped out soon as it happens...

What? He wrinkles up his face in perplexity.

The Korsakoff's, Mounty. I think the doctors called you, that day they took me off the train...when I was going to you, after Carol...

You couldn't walk, they said.

Well, yes, and now I can, I am exceptional in that. What happened to my brain, however, fits the typical, the classical, you know...

Ah, yes, I think I looked it up. I usually do... But how far back...the lapse...?

Oh, only recent memory is impaired. I do remember husband, children, the multiplication tables, almost. I never had a very firm grip on them to start... But there were blackouts soon as I was in my thirties, and I neglected, then, to keep a notebook, as I do now, ha, ha! She laughs, resuming her hostess voice; the conversation coming close to places that might set him against her.

So it was magic to you, then science, a classic recapitulation, she says; but not for me; I stopped off somewhere short of science, but it wasn't magic either...Curious. Maybe women don't, you know, recapitulate...If you were after gold, then what was I...? A horse, I think. I would have liked a horse I didn't have to make up in my head. I dreamed of one with gears and motors to make him run. He didn't either eat or shit, two things that Lutie objected to in horses.

Zeppelins... Mounty muses. The technology of lighter than air ships was the most promising thing around when I was in the first and second grade; by the time I was in boarding school, they'd given up the whole caboodle. World War II. And no one ever equaled the Germans. It might have been a different story if they'd won. These cargo planes they have today, most inefficient transport ever was invented... Like giant ocean liners, the zeppelins they had projected. Room for every luxury...

I traveled once, in one of these jets they have, he went on; I didn't know where they thought you were supposed to put your arms and legs for six or seven hours...Never traveled again.

Horses for her, then, and Zeppelins for him. As far back as grammar school they'd parted ways, she thinks. Can I have magnified those early years out of all proportion? Mounty had been more animated talking with Charles about antique music boxes, than just now, for all her urgency.

As usual, he'd sought to settle her puzzlement by one of his pronouncements: A classic recapitulation; that had been their childhood for him.

A classic dipsomaniac, she'd been called by that man in the Newton meeting. Well that had the merit of being true. She's not sure about Mounty's pronouncement; and now he's dozing off.

Oh, but I am a hard woman! He came. He has not taken a drink, or very little, or his hands would not be shaking. How can I come at him with these matters over which I obsess because they are the only intact memories I have, and expect him, who hasn't necessarily thought about his childhood in years, to have ready answers for me?

Forgive me Mounty, she breathes.

Umph, he says.

Later, later, Clarissa Dalloway told herself in the midst of her party. We have tomorrow to talk. We have years to talk, Henrietta Rose tells herself, and turns her attention back to her party.

Barbara de la Cuesta taught and worked as a journalist in South America, and has long been a teacher of English as a Second Language and Spanish. Out of this experience came her two prize winning novels, *The Spanish Teacher*, winner of the Gival Press Award in 2007, and *Rosa*, winner of the Driftless Novella Prize from Brain Mill Press in 2017. Fellowships in fiction from the Massachusetts Artists' Foundation, and the New Jersey Council on the Arts, as well as residencies at the Ragdale Foundation, The Virginia Center, and the Millay Colony, have allowed her to complete these novels. She has also published two collections of poetry with Finishing Line Press, and her collection of short stories, *The Place Where Judas Lost his Boots*, has recently won The Brighthorse Prize for short fiction.